Easy Victories

Easy Victories

James Trowbridge

Houghton Mifflin Company Boston
1973

FIRST PRINTING V

ISBN: 0-395-15569-x
Library of Congress Catalog Card Number: 72-9018
Printed in the United States of America

To all who went there

The Leg Irons

With hungry mouth open like a wicked monster,
Each night the irons devour the legs of people:
The jaws grip the right leg of every prisoner:
Only the left is free to bend and stretch.

Yet there is one thing stranger in this world:
People rush in to place their legs in irons.
Once they are shackled, they can sleep in peace.
Otherwise they would have no place to lay their heads.

Prison Diary, written between
28 August 1942 and 16 September 1943
by Nguyen that Thanh, variously
known as Nguyen ai Quoc or
Ho chi Minh, Vietnamese politician

Easy Victories

Saigon, RVN

I

FROM THE TIN-ROOFED PORCH in front of the mortuary one could see the old stone fort the French had built. The Americans used the magazines now to store sheets and C-rations. Behind the fort was the incinerator where the greenies burned the clothing from the dead. Beyond that was a small dispensary where the Air Force corpsmen gave immunizations, and sometimes long queues of men waited silently in the heat and the dust and the drone of flies for their injections.

The drums of formaldehyde were stacked in tiers on the graveled space between, rust already flaking through the black paint and the wood of crates splintered from hasty shipment, careless handling or just indifference. The trucks entered the yard beside the mortuary and the rubberized bags were lifted out by indifferent men. Other trucks drove away with aluminum coffins stacked neatly on blue trailers. But no one in the silent lines looked even casually toward the mortuary or the trucks coming and going. Above it all was the smell, the stench which was death and piss and blood from the body bags, and formaldehyde, and the faint, fine gray ash from the incinerator filtering down on everything to blend with the reddish dust which lay on the buildings, the magazines, the small tin-roofed porch, the barrels of formaldehyde, the coffins and the living.

II

There was a neatly lettered chart prominently displayed in the outer office:

AVERAGE PROCESSING TIME PER REMAINS
Receipt and Verification of Identity — 30 min.
Embalming Operations — 4 hrs. 15 min.°
Preservation of Body Tissues — 8 hrs.
Packing — 10 min.
Out Processing — 30 min.
Total — 13 hrs. 25 min.
° Severely mangled, charred or badly decomposed remains can require 10 minutes to 6 hours depending on the condition.

The Vietnamese exercise boys preparing to exercise their diminutive horses found him at the Hippodrome, found him in the tall grass, crumpled in the sagging mortar and bricks against the wall which straggled between the road and the track. His hands tied behind his back with commo wire so tight it was lost in transparent puffiness, and his head stitched crudely with bootlaces where his stomach had been. Flies gathered in one gigantic clot on the stump of neck. Along the Hippodrome wall out past the perimeter fence which surrounded Tan son Nhut, out past the old Legionnaire barracks which were deserted now, and the Legionnaire cemetery which was not, with its neat rows of white crosses almost hidden now in the unkept grasses.

B.D. had just come from the pale green rooms behind the office. He had seen the civilian morticians and their Vietnamese assistants open the body bags and slide what used

2

to be men onto steel tables waist high to them above the floor. He had seen certain bodies go back to the reefers, big walk-in refrigerators of the kind some restaurants have, either because the embalming room was full or because no one could yet decide who or what a particular body had been.

B.D. folded another stick of gum into his mouth and steadily regarded the Army captain in the starched jungle fatigues behind the issue metal desk the government had bought. "I want him now," he said through the wad of gum.

"You can't have him now," the Army captain said. "The tissues haven't set. I can't release a body until at least eight hours after it's been embalmed, look at the sign."

"I want him now. I got to have him now. You've pickled him. That's enough. He won't know the difference."

The Army captain: "Why didn't you get him here sooner? You don't know what a hell of a time we have keeping morticians. Another job like this and I'll have to ship another man back to the States in a strait jacket. Sweet Jesus, we bring in enough weirdos of our own without you complicating things."

When the embalming is done the bodies lie and wait throughout the night for the formaldehyde to fix. B.D. had seen the bodies carried into the packing room, where other men in sleeveless smocks put the bodies in plastic bags. First they put in strips of cotton and absorbent powder, then pads of cotton on what had been eyes and pads on what had been crotches. Then the vacuumer took over and sucked out the air in the bag and the soft plastic crinkled down around the body like a package of vegetables in a supermarket. Then someone else in a green smock, perhaps one of the Vietnamese helpers, wrapped masking tape around the top of the bag to preserve the vacuum.

Generally the Vietnamese used more tape than was needed — the Vietnamese were always using more of everything than was needed — but then, that was the way Vietnamese were. B.D. used to joke that saying "stupid Vietnamese" was being redundant. That was a long time ago, before he came to know the Vietnamese. But people still said that about the Vietnamese, and every time they said it they chuckled, as if they had invented some intensely funny anecdote.

"It's bad enough you Embassy people coming in here and getting priority over regular Army people, but I'll be goddamned if I'll let you take a body before it's properly took care of. I've got the reputation of my outfit to think of."

B.D. glanced at his watch and perspired quietly. Great half-circles of sweat extended from his armpits almost to his belt. He tugged up his trousers and stuffed in his flopping shirttail. But it sagged out again. "Nobody's going to see him," he said mildly, but the look in the Army captain's eyes did not change so he leaned across the desk and without asking the Army captain picked up the telephone and dialed the Embassy exchange. He almost muffed it because he was always forgetting how to dial the Embassy from Tan son Nhut, or anywhere else for that matter (the communications people were always changing the numbers), but he did not want to ask the captain for a telephone directory.

He waited while the phone rang and rang and then someone at the switchboard answered and he gave his special number. After a while the Chief answered and he talked to the Chief in a few terse words and then was silent while the Chief talked to him. B.D. leaned across the desk and picked a cigarette out of the pack on the captain's blotter. He spoke a few more words into the telephone, then spelled the Army captain's name, reading it from the captain's name tape in black Tu Do Street sewn letters on the breast of his fatigues, nodded, said "yessir," then hung up and lit the cigarette with the captain's lighter.

He stood in front of the government issue desk and looked around, but he did not need to do that to know what the room contained because he had seen it before. Nor did he need to look out the window because he knew what was out there, too. Mostly he was waiting for the phone to ring so he could take Cresap's body and meet the plane and pick up the new man and then go home and take a shower and sit under his fan, which was a hell of a lot better than the puny air conditioner that was slugging stale air about the room.

B.D. looked at his watch which was covered with a film of sweat. Two minutes had passed. He guessed it would take the Chief another two minutes, depending on the telephones, that is. Christ, you could never get anything done in Saigon because of the telephones. Who ever heard of fighting a war without adequate telephones? God Almighty, maybe they would fight the next one in Bangkok. At least they had telephones there. Better hotels, too.

The clerk in the office was trying to type, but he kept glancing at first the Army captain and then B.D., and he was not getting anything done. But that was all right with B.D. because the clerk and the captain, in fact the whole frigging Army, were paid by someone other than him, and he did not care. It was all right with the clerk, too, because he had managed to snag a plush job as a typist instead of going to the boonies. He was thankful for that every time a truckload of bodies came in.

B.D. smoked and crushed out the butt in the clean ashtray on the captain's desk and continued to stand in the middle of the room without saying anything because he knew that sooner or later the phone would ring and he could take Cresap and he would not have to argue with the

Army or this particular captain again for a while. And then the phone rang and he said, without lifting his eyes from the ashtray, "That's for you"; but the clerk answered anyway (he had been trained to do that) and then handed the phone to the captain, who spoke his name into the receiver. Then he listened and did not say anything though the muscles in his jaws bunched and he swallowed once or twice but that was all.

Then he said "yessir" in much the same way B.D. had done when he talked to the Chief. "That was MACV. They said I'm to give you the body."

B.D. nodded and reached out to take another cigarette. "I figured that's what they'd say."

The captain turned to his clerk. "Tell the men to get that civilian's body, the one they found out by the Hippodrome, ready to go now. Tell them MACV says it's all right and we can do it this time."

"I'll need a coffin, too."

"I'm not authorized to furnish you with a coffin. You'll have to take him in a body bag."

"He can't go back to the States in a bag."

"Then you'll have to get a transfer case somewhere else."

B.D. sighed and reached for the telephone and began dialing for the Embassy, but the captain stopped him. "Okay, you can have your goddamned coffin."

The clerk reentered the room and the captain shuffled through a desk drawer, then flipped a pad of forms at the clerk. "Fix me a hand receipt for a transfer case." He glanced at the form when the clerk had typed it, then thrust it at B.D. "Put your name at the bottom and either return the case or bring me another. I'm signed for them, you know."

"You'll be long gone from here by the time anybody

makes an inventory. That's one thing you've got plenty of, coffins."

III

B.D. did not see the plane land. Planes were always taking off and landing at Tan son Nhut. Military planes, civilian planes. He paid little attention to them unless he was supposed to ride in one. For he did things when and only when he felt they were right and necessary to the harmony of things. And he worked harder for whatever reason he thought he had than for anything mere mortals could hope to offer him. Right now he had to see that Cresap, or what had been Cresap, got on the right plane and the new man got off another. He bought a pack of cigarettes from a hawker outside the terminal, close to the roped-off area where the R and R buses waited. He paid sixty piastres for them and the pack came out of a carton with the Army and Air Force Exchange Service price stamp still on it. A Vietnamese Canh Sat policeman wearing dingy gray trousers and a revolver with a rusting butt in a faded holster originally designed for another type of pistol stood nearby and looked bored. Some women were squatting beside their shoulder poles, trying to sell pineapple and sugar cane cubes, holding up miniature umbrellas of the fruit skewered on bamboo splinters, the cakes of ice in their glass-sided containers melting and forming puddles in the dust. A fly, too gorged on sugar water to lift off, droned his wings in the puddle, and after a while one of the women spat betel juice on him.

B.D. heard the plane announced and knew he was late, but J. H. Christ, he had to take care of Cresap. The new man would just have to wait, goddamn him. The Vietnamese driver sat on the right side of the seat where B.D. had pushed him when he drove away from the mortuary. The Vietnamese was picking his teeth with a frayed matchstick and scratching his stomach through his shirt with a dirty fingernail. B.D. backed the Embassy station wagon up to the entry gate to the left of the VIP lounge and went to find the Pan Am ground crew. An American military policeman eyed the car, but B.D. pointed to the Embassy plates.

Stupid sonabitch, he thought. He should check the car even if it does have an Embassy tag. For all the fuck he knows it could be a VC trick. But even as he thought it he knew he would be extremely put out if the MP asked him for identification.

B.D. found the Pan Am ground crew and showed the foreman his papers. The foreman tried to argue, then cursed and dropped his shoulders in fatigue and defeat. He beckoned for one of his crew to bring a hand truck. "It's all I got can handle a load that big," he said. He was a sergeant moonlighting after a ten-hour shift in order to get enough money to send some home to his wife after meeting the expenses of supporting a house girl in Gia Dinh.

They went back through the terminal, and B.D. thought he saw his man standing over by customs. At least this fellow looked properly tired, and B.D. could see the stubble of beard even at a distance. The man was even wearing a heavy Stateside suit, though the coat was under his arm. But B.D. had to do first things first. The foreman and one of his crewmen wrestled the big aluminum coffin out of the back of the station wagon and strapped it to the hand truck.

"Which end is the head?"

"Damn if I know. It don't make any difference. Just get him on that plane." The Vietnamese driver had not offered to help them with the unloading, and now he was standing idly by the hood, mutely flicking at the dust on the car with the strange feather duster all drivers carried and with which they all flicked at the dust when they had nothing else to do. "Drive it over underneath the shade, and be ready to come over to the terminal when I need you," B.D. said.

"Yah," the driver said. He never interrupted his dusting or turned his head to indicate he had heard, his only word of acknowledgment almost lost in the confusion of the terminal's traffic and the high whine of a cargo jet trying to lift off in the superheated air.

B.D. accompanied the procession back through the terminal and showed his papers to the head Vietnamese customs official. The customs official glanced at the papers without reading them, though he pretended to. B.D. doubted if he could even read, but the stamps on the documents looked official enough.

Christ, but it's hot, he thought. B.D. wanted a beer badly and toyed briefly with the idea of buying a Ba-me-ba from one of the Howard Johnson stands. Naw, he finally decided, too much talk about glass in the beer. He wiped his face with one hand and felt for a handkerchief, but found none so he pulled out his shirt tail and wiped his face with that. The big, meaty freckles which bridged his nose stood out like splotches of huge summer rain on a sidewalk. He could smell himself quite plainly.

He found the new man sitting on an unpended suitcase and leaning against a pillar in front of the Air Vietnam ticket office. The new man's suit was wrinkled and badly stained from a coffee spill. His tie had been roughly pulled loose and the button on the wilted collar was open. The tinge of blond whiskers showed faint on his chin. Altogether he looked like someone who was very tired and out of humor. He was the man B.D. had seen earlier at customs, and he resembled the picture B.D. had seen before leaving the office on Han Thuyen Street.

The man regarded him quizzically through eyes the color of an old shirt faded yellow. The tip of his nose was sunburned already. He guessed who B.D. was even though B.D. knew the man had never seen a picture of him. "The Embassy."

B.D. nodded. "Let me see your passport, please."

The man picked up his coat and rummaged through several pockets. He finally located the passport and handed it to B.D. B.D. compared the picture with the man for a moment, then gave it back. The new man slipped the passport into a side pocket of his coat. It did not go in all the way. Americans were always careless with their passports.

"I'm Knox," the new man said, as if expecting the mere mention of his name to strike some responsive chord in B.D. He looked invulnerable, his face lean with the confidence and self-assurance ingrained from habitually possessing young and enjoying long. He had something of the look of the fraternity brother about him still; he radiated the values of the fraternity, drinking properly, women and a good time. "Why weren't you here earlier?"

B.D. disliked the man immediately. He had not belonged to a fraternity. But he held out his hand. Knox took it and B.D. saw the tiny rivulets of grime already caught in the folds of the neck, and the fatigue in the yellow eyes. "I'm Drummond. First name is Bouledogue. My father was a Frenchman, second generation, but he had a sense of humor. People at the office call me B.D." Knox took his hand away. "Welcome to Vietnam," B.D. said, "the only place in the world where you can have diarrhea and a dusty asshole at the same time."

Knox smiled weakly. "That supposed to be a joke?"

"It won't take you long to find out. Most people get the Ho Chis within a day or two after they first get here."

"Ho Chis?"

"The trots, man. You know, the plain old-fashioned shits." Christ, B.D. thought. "Don't let anybody get between you and a bathroom. You might embarrass yourself. One of the troops who just went upcountry had it so bad he's still wearing a Kotex." He glanced at Knox's suitcase with distaste. It was Samsonite. Very new and very expensive. It was even unscuffed.

Knox was still sitting on the upended suitcase. He had not risen to shake hands. "What's your job?" He said.

"I'm responsible for O and E. You got any more suitcases?"

"What's O and E?"

"Odds and ends. What about your other suitcases?"

"Three more. They're on that baggage rack over there." Knox pulled some baggage claim checks from his shirt pocket and held them toward B.D. B.D. ignored them.

"Point them out." B.D. stepped heavily over the railing into the baggage area. But he saw Knox's suitcases right away. They matched the one on which he was sitting. B.D. slid one under the railing and picked up the other two.

"I never did get a customs clearance."

B.D. ignored him. "I'm ready to get out of this place." His shirt was one sodden, shapeless mess now. A bead of sweat formed on the end of his nose, but he did not try to wipe it away. B.D. dropped the two suitcases he was carrying. Immediately two Vietnamese men in loose, dirty overalls ran over. One picked up both suitcases. B.D. pushed him away. "Di di mau, get the hell out of here."

Knox was silent.

"I lost a bag that way my first day incountry. You'd better be glad you got somebody to look after you." B.D. picked up one suitcase, then another reluctantly. Knox was holding an attaché case B.D. had not seen before. It must have been behind the other suitcase, the one Knox had been sitting on. Most of the contract agents fresh out of the intelligence school carried attaché cases when they first came out. B.D. should have expected it.

They stumbled out into the searing brightness of the parking lot. The Embassy car was parked in the sparse shade of the trees on the far side of the parking lot, but the driver was nowhere in sight. It did no good to curse. B.D. sighed and began trudging across the shimmering parking lot, the heat coming painfully to him through his shoes from the viscous pavement. He did not look back to see if Knox was behind him. He reached the car breathing hard, dropped the bags and called for the driver. Men came out of the station wagon by the right front door and shambled to the back.

Men knuckled his eyes and blew his nose, using his pinched fingers. He wiped mucus on one trouser leg. B.D. pulled the keys from the ignition and threw them at Men. They hit the Vietnamese on the chest and fell to the buckled pavement with a briefly musical sound. Men flashed a smile bright with gold-yellowed teeth. "Yes," he said.

"Were you listening to the radio?"

"Yes." Men smiled again.

"You filthy cocksucker."

Knox walked up with the other bag and his attaché case. His coat was under his arm and B.D. could not see his passport. "How have you stood the tour if little things like this get to you?"

"This bastard was probably playing the radio all the time I was in the terminal. If he was playing it while I was at the mortuary the battery may be run down and we'll have to push this wreck unless we're lucky and get a push from some GI." B.D. unlocked the rear baggage door. "Sure you got your passport?"

Knox slapped at the pockets of his coat. "Damn it, I know I put it back."

"It probably fell out, better go back and find it. The Chief won't like it if you lose your passport your first day in-country."

Knox flushed but said nothing. He walked back toward the terminal. B.D. loaded the suitcases into the rear, then slid behind the wheel and turned the ignition key. There was a hesitant moment while the starter ground and did not catch, then the engine spluttered into life. B.D. raced the engine, more than was good for it.

Knox returned. He had his passport in one hand. "I dropped it about fifty yards back."

B.D. nodded. "Better put it somewhere you can't lose it." He raced the engine again. Men was standing by ineffectually.

"Get in," B.D. said. The Vietnamese got in the back seat. Knox sat by B.D.

"What's so upsetting about leaving the radio on?"

"Plenty. Batteries don't last long in this heat. One of these bastards left the ignition on one night during a big blowout at Ky's palace. He was driving one of those Department of Defense bigwigs, might even have been McNamara himself, I don't remember. Anyway, we had to push the sonabitch off. Up a damn big curving drive. In the rain, with the cocksucker really bombed, laughing his frigging head off." B.D. drove forward, turning sharply in front of a R and R bus, then right out of the parking lot, heading toward the first checkpoint and the cutoff to Cach Mang Street.

"The Viets are fine examples of parthenogenesis," B.D. said. He was driving with one hand on the steering wheel and the other hand to his mouth, biting at a fingernail. Knox heard him indistinctly.

"What do you mean?" His stomach went suddenly queasy as B.D. nudged up to an old Vietnamese on a bicycle and blew the horn. The Vietnamese veered away without looking back. A moment later he was riding only inches away from the car as they passed, his eyes fixed on something only he could see.

B.D. nudged the rear of a pedicab and blew the horn again, then swerved to the right and passed with a burst of speed, slowing abruptly to avoid an ox cart filled with rough-sawn lumber. "I mean development of an egg cell without fertilization by sperm. In short, I mean they're bastards." He was still either picking his teeth or biting his fingernails.

"I thought we were out here to win the hearts and minds of these people."

"You can screw that. The only way to get through to the Viets is to get them by the balls. Then their hearts and minds got to follow."

Knox braced against the floorboard as an old Renault bumped out of a side alley and turned into the line of traffic. B.D. veered around it. A three-wheeled motorcycle with a metal basket in front and two Vietnamese girls in it passed them in a steady stream of blue exhaust. Knox's eyes smarted. "What kind of motorcycle is that?"

"It's a cyclo. Most people call them motorized junks. Only vehicle in the world uses the passenger as the bumper."

"They look dangerous."

"Everything's dangerous over here."

"You don't think we should be out here."

"I didn't say that. All I said was, 'Get them by the balls

and their hearts gotta follow.' Hell's bells, man, you think these people are ready for democracy? Ask one of them. They can't even spell it. Things like democracy, liberty, all that pretty stuff in the speeches is so much crap to them. They can't think any further than the next bowl of rice."

"Why do you stay out here if that's the case?"

"The Agency pays me pretty well. Besides that, I've got a responsibility to myself to see this war through." B.D. laughed, and it was high, almost a giggle, not what you would expect from a man his size. "The fighter pilots and Special Forces types say this is our only war and we've got to nurse it along; maybe I stay just to see pricks like them get their noses out of joint."

They were past all the checkpoints now. They rattled over a connecting road in the process of being paved, though great potholes stood out in the gravel, and they had to slow down for one especially large hole puddled with rainwater. They were through an intersection then, by a large hospital painted white with symmetrical crosses in red on the roof. They traveled along a fairly broad street lined on both sides with villas behind high walls and new hotels and the skeletons of other buildings standing in rickety scaffolding. "This is Cach Mang," B.D. said. "It becomes something else up ahead. At a bridge. That's where Saigon really begins."

"Do you think we're winning the war? No one back in the States seems to know. Some team comes out here and makes a report that everything is rosy. McNamara says the war will be won in another year. Then you catch the evening news."

"We're bombing the hell out of the North."

"Then you think we'll get the North Vietnamese to the conference table?"

"Shit no. All we'll do with the bombing is get us to the conference table. If that happens we'll probably lose the war no matter what anybody in Washington says. And we won't be defeated by Ho chi Minh or Nguyen vo Giap; we'll be beaten by CBS and the *New York Times.*"

"You sound like the war's getting you down."

"Sometimes it gets to you when you see a lot of people getting rich off the black market. If I had a mind to I could make a couple of thousand in the black market every month, real easy."

The station wagon rattled over a rough stretch where the street had been dug up to lay a new water pipe. "I thought that sort of thing went on only between the Asiatics, you know, stealing stuff from the ports."

"That goes on all the time. It's small potatoes. Every now and then Ky gets some pressure put on him when a big congressional junket comes through in a day. Ky sends around some trucks to load up all the stuff they can find on the streets. 'Course, everybody's had plenty of time to move things and they're back on the street two days later. All the congressmen who've come out have been pricks. You know, get their pictures in the paper wearing jungle fatigues and inspecting some pig farm or new well. Stay in the Caravelle every night, then leave. Anyway, the big money is in currency manipulation. You can get as high as one hundred fifty to one, sometimes even one hundred seventy to one hundred MPC for US green. Then you convert the MPC back to green and start all over again."

"What's MPC?"

"Christ, man, didn't you change your money to scrip at the airport?"

"Was I supposed to? And what's scrip?"

"MPC. Scrip. Same difference. Everybody over here

gets paid in military pay certificates. MPC. You have to change your US dollars into MPC when you arrive, and you can't deal with the Vietnamese in anything but piastres." B.D. struck a match to a cigarette and sucked in the smoke. "No sweat, you can change your green at the office. Wait till you get a look at it. The ten-buck MPC has a woman on the back that looks exactly like Jackie Kennedy. Christ help me."

He laughed, a high, almost obscene laugh, showing gross uneven teeth stained brown from cigarette smoke. Smoking too much, perspiring too easily, dressing badly, always tearing something, drinking only beer and swilling that; but very sensitive, dedicated, though trying not to show it, and extremely competent. He would be assigned to help Knox learn the trade, though neither knew it just then, and had either of them known he would not have been particularly pleased. For B.D. was certain in his assumption that man would be destroyed by the gods, or lack of them — whatever — it really made no difference to him, but he still retained his dignity as a man, a human entity, and that was the one, the sole and only material mortal treasure not hostage to fortune.

"But how can you make so much money in the black market?" They drove over a bridge with a small weather-stained sign which was lettered RAN SAIGON. The tide was out and the exposed black mud smelled like a slaughter-house long decayed. The smell hit Knox like a physical blow. B.D. did not seem to notice. Knox looked out at the shanties built over the mud flats, rickety boards, tarpaper, bits of packing crates topped with rusty tin and standing on stilts. A keelboat with a large red eye painted on the bow was careened against the bank and a Vietnamese up to his knees in the black mud was burning off barnacles with a smudge torch. Then they were across the bridge and past the little guardhouse with the ubiquitous policeman in white shirt and gray trousers.

"But how can you make so much money in the black market?" Knox said. Again.

B.D. lit another cigarette from the stub of the last one. Everyone told him he smoked too much. He knew Knox was probably already thinking that. B.D. blew smoke out the window. Men made a noise in the back and B.D. gave the butt to the Vietnamese. "You take your green to one of the Indians or Chinese downtown. They buy the green with MPC because they can't use the MPC, but the dollar is the one currency that's good all over the world. Anywhere. Any time. If you haggle right you can get one fifty, one seventy MPC for every hundred dollars in green. You convert the green back to MPC and do the whole thing over again. Anywhere you have an occupation army you have the currency market.

"The Army had a guy working in the finance cage at the R and R center. He made almost a million bucks in the time he was here and then some CID agent blew it. They didn't advise the kid of his rights and the government couldn't prosecute him. All's that they could do was sic the Internal Revenue on him. IRS got seventy-one per cent. There was some ass-chewing at CID, let me tell you. But the kid finked on a whole bunch of people. He knew a lot who'd been changing. Even a colonel or two in the bunch. MACV had the whole thing hushed up."

They passed a park surrounded by a high fence with pickets made from long iron spikes. A sandbagged guardhouse like a small pagoda was set at the corner of a hill, and then a long palacelike building slid into view. "That's Gia Long Palace. Call it Independence Palace. Most of the playboy correspondents do. Shows how much they know. Ky lives there now. Diem lived there, too. That wing over there is the one that got bombed before the big coup. Those were some days. It wasn't so bad before Johnson got scared and ran in all the troops."

"You were here then?"

"Yeah, I've been here since sixty. Makes me the oldest man in the Station except for one old OSS man upcountry who's always talking about how he knew Ho chi Minh during World War Two."

"What keeps you here?"

"You might say that in my perverse way I like these people. They're stupid as shit but they're likable." He turned to the Vietnamese in the back seat. "Right, Charlie?"

The Vietnamese turned his attention from the palace for a moment and nodded gravely. His face grinned for an instant, then foolishly, shrewdly subsided.

"We call him Charlie because the white mice arrested him for a VC suspect. They couldn't hang him with anything, but all the same they've got his family hidden away somewhere, either in Binh Thuy or Phu Quoc Island. He's been on his best behavior since coming to work for us."

"Well I'll be a sonofabitch."

"Yeah, you'll be that all right," B.D. said, "and more before Vietnam gets through with you."

IV

B.D. walked down the darkened hallway with Knox in tow. He nodded at a Vietnamese in a small room with only a desk-top lamp and a fan whirring furiously overhead. The Vietnamese rose and half bowed. There was a framed citation on the wall behind him attesting to his excellence as an interpreter. The Americans were always good at giving out certificates for almost anything. The Vietnamese smiled nervously, but they had already passed and did not see. "Mr. Khiem," B.D. said. "The Chief's interpreter."

He knocked once on a plain wooden door and without waiting opened it. Mister Balfour looked up from his desk. He was pouring a can of Coke into a glass of ice. The Coke foamed over and some of it spilled down the glass and speckled the papers on his desk. "How many times have I told you to knock before coming in here?"

"I knocked."

"Then wait until I tell you to come in."

"I knew you were going to tell me to come in, so I came in. I brought the new man."

Mister Balfour set the glass on another stack of papers. "Knock next time, goddamn it, and wait for an answer. Knox, is it? You look a lot like your father. How is he?"

"Well. He's retired now, living in Bethesda and acting as a consultant to State whenever they want him. When did you know my father?"

"We were together in the Foreign Service before I came to work for the Agency. Almost everyone in the Service had a kind word for him."

"Particularly after he made Ambassador."

Mister Balfour looked sharply at Knox. He brushed at his trousers with a handkerchief, then motioned with it toward a chair. "Sit down."

Knox did. B.D. sat on a rattan sofa across the office.

"Even before he made Ambassador. Everyone who met your father liked him. His being picked for Ambassador had nothing to do with all that. It was one of those cases which was strictly a matter of merit." Mister Balfour took a sip of Coke, tilting his head back like a chicken drinking water, and his glasses lenses were mirrors of silver from the light.

"B.D. can give you a general view of our operations and take you around to the various department heads for some more detailed briefings. I like to see everybody as they come in or leave and have a chat with them, pick their brains, you might say, for any new slants or information they might have. Something I learned firsthand from Mr. Dulles. It's a good thing to remember if you're ever picked to run a station."

Knox inclined his head. "I'll remember."

"Good. I know you will." Mister Balfour swiveled in his chair. "Now." He cleared his throat and took another sip of Coke. "We have you slated for one of the upcountry offices. Phan Rang, to be exact. You'll be needed there, particularly since you contracted for Operation Phoenix work. The office is understaffed and we just lost a man from there so you'll be doubly welcomed by the office. You'll have the whole Cam Ranh Bay area as well, but there's nothing too much there. The Air Force services it and you pick up any information they might accidentally stumble over. It's a VC Secret Zone and R and R center area. They don't bother the base there and the base doesn't bother them." He turned to B.D. "You can put him up for a night or two, can't you?"

B.D. was lost in a cloud of cigarette smoke. "If I have to," he said finally.

Then back to Knox: "I don't know what you heard in the training school at Washington. But you can forget it. This is a pretty straightforward intelligence-gathering operation, except for Phoenix, which is just getting off the ground. That's how I'm going to use you primarily, but you'll get plenty of briefings on that later. The Army's in it with us and they're good at briefings. They'll brief you to death. If wars were won by briefings, the Army'd have this one in the bag.

"Just remember there're no James Bonds in this kind of business. No pretty spies trying to get into your pants. No roll-over cameras, no one-time pads, no miniature radio transmitters, no fast cars. Just plain old-fashioned vetting and writing it up by the book, lots of IIRs to write, God yes, lots of those —"

"What's an IIR?"

Mister Balfour put down his Coke glass and looked reflectively at Knox. "You don't know what an IIR is? Just what *did* they teach you at school about report writing?"

"Well, they showed us how to make an EEI but no one said anything about an IIR."

Mister Balfour sighed. "Trust the school to be two years behind the times. An IIR is the same thing an EEI used to be."

"Back at the school they're still calling them EEIs."

"Khristonacrutch, man, get it through your skull that you can't go by anything that fuckin' school taught. This is the real thing out here, no old fairies prancing around telling you how they did it when Donovan had all those wild-ass schemes to liberate the French and arm them with slingshots made from old condoms. The real world's out there and it's got you by the scroats unless you bugger it first."

"Yessir."

Mister Balfour finished the Coke in the glass and poured more from the can, being careful this time to stop before it foamed over. "Anyway, there'll be lots of IIRs to write and everybody from the Ambassador on down wants a good job. That's his policy, and it goes without saying that because it's his policy it's also my policy. You've got to always keep in mind that these reports go to MACV as well as our own internal distribution, the Ambassador's staff, that new DIA thing McNamara started and of course State. So they've got to look professional. You'd be surprised how many times some general at MACV or an area specialist in Foggy Bottom distrusts a report because it isn't neat enough, professional-looking enough."

"Aren't the other intelligence services getting distribution, too?"

"Yes, oh hell yes. And they're sending us data, some of it's good stuff. I'm not knocking them, but we're the ones with the reputation to keep us. And naturally we don't want the other shops to swing onto some intelligence which they can use to upstage us. So if you get some really good information let us know about it here and don't put it out to the Army or Air Force types until we've had a chance to pass on it."

The air conditioner was slipping cool air almost unnoticed into the room. Knox felt suddenly cold, then hot again. He sneezed.

"Bless you," Mister Balfour said. "You'd better get cleaned up. Take a couple of aspirin as well. A lot of our people coming over get colds their first week here. Keep them for a long time, too. Something about the change of climate and doing it so quickly. Just don't get too hot or too cold too quickly. I like my people to stay healthy." Mister Balfour got up from behind his cluttered desk and for the first time offered his hand. Knox stood and took it. The clasp was limp and somewhat sweaty despite the cool air. He could see that Mister Balfour was not wearing an undershirt.

"I'd like to know some more about this Operation Phoenix thing."

"Later, later. One of the section chiefs runs it as his personal baby, more or less. I don't know a great deal about it myself. Remember, we're just seeing if it's going to fly. My job is to stay on top of the overall big picture. B.D. will take you around to the right people. When you write your father tell him that I send my regards. Tell him I wish we had him over in the Embassy now. He knows about the problems we have to put up with."

"I'm sure."

Mister Balfour dismissed them with a wave of his hand. "Feel completely free to drop in and see me any time. That's what I'm here for. Support the field in every way. That's something else Mr. Dulles always told me." He went back to his desk.

B.D. opened the door and they stepped through. They passed the small office where the Vietnamese interpreter again got to his feet, half-smiling, half-bowing. But they were already gone and did not see him, though he was smiling long after they had left.

V

Knox had worn a coat and tie, though B.D. had tried to argue him out of it. They left B.D.'s villa behind the larger villa on the street which ran by the Cirque Sportif and took one of the ubiquitous blue-and-dusty-cream Renault taxis to the Rex BOQ, where they ate in the American-style restaurant run by the Army and afterward walked downstairs because the electricity had failed and the elevator was out of service.

"You tired from all that traveling or do you want to see some of the Vietnamese night life?" B.D. asked as they stood in the sweltering dusk outside the Rex.

They turned toward the Constituent Assembly Building, the drab white tin-roofed hulk which had once housed the Saigon Opera. Knox had sneezed several times during dinner and he sneezed now. His throat was tight and he felt slightly dizzy. "I'm not too tired if you've got anything worthwhile to show me."

"Well for starters I can show you a pile of cat shit you're about to step in."

"The correct terminology is 'scats.' Cat scats."

"Cat shit," B.D. said. "Then for the really big show, I can point out the Vietnamese Marine Memorial. You already passed the heap of junk which was the Vietnamese Air Force Memorial."

"Where was that?"

"Just outside the Rex."

"It didn't look like it had much to do with aviation. It was just a stack of metal to me."

"I think it must have been the first plane the Viets crashed. Back to my original topic. If you notice, this memorial has two Marines charging full tilt at the Assembly Building. And as with most Viets, one is directly behind the other. No one knows if the one in back is hiding or pushing the other one. Anyway, it's pure Vietnamese."

"Are you saying these people have no culture?"

"No, I don't mean that. They've got a lot of history, more than three thousand years' worth. I've read a lot about it. They had heroes like Le Loi, the Truong Sisters, Truong minh Ky, but that's all in the past and few Viets know much about them anymore. The Government puts up statues ever so often, but the average Nguyen van Smith doesn't know them from Adam. Give them a bowl of rice, like I said, and forget that crap about history and freedom. The French did a good job of beating history out of them. These little bastards claim they hate the French, but try to talk to the ones got any education at all and they speak French."

"Well, where are these places you're going to take me?"

"Not down Tu Do, that's for damn sure. That's where the GIs hang out. Commercialized. They got some broads down there who can torque your gut wrench out of shape."

"Where, then?"

"I'll take you to some of the quieter places on Cach Mang or over in Da Kao. The hero boys don't have much time to score when they hit town so most of them end up on Tu Do."

So they hailed another Renault taxi, riding away from the center of the city and down a wide street past a huge bulking silence in the evening sky which B.D. said was the Saigon Basilica, past another building further down which was going to be (one day) the new American Embassy, then left at the big Shell Oil Building and on into Da Kao. Past the soccer fields and a pile of rubbish tumbled into the street where flies swarmed in the waning headlights, over the carcass of a rat as long as an arm which graced the top of the rubbish in which a young Vietnamese boy was raking with a rusty coat hanger. A woman squatted stoically on the sidewalk nearby and chattered across an alley in her guttural voice while she held her child's buttocks spread apart in her hands and the child defecated in the street.

Past the little shops which sold wicker and wire wreaths and crosses and other trappings of ceremonial mortality, closed and rusty-shuttered now with the metal doors which criss-crossed like folding gates, to a busy intersection unreal in the too bright light of neon proclaiming rice cookers, health foods, patent medicines, Perlon toothpaste and bars. The taxi came to a stop at the curb and B.D. pointed to the meter and asked how much, but the driver twisted the handle to indicate the meter did not work and said "On hundret p," but B.D. laughed and peeled two twenty-piastre notes from a wad in his pocket and dropped them on the front seat. He got out and motioned for Knox to follow.

"Damn bastard must think he's dealing with a rookie. All of them say their meters don't work. Screw him, he can get rich off somebody else." The taxi, which was just like any other taxi in Saigon, including the meter which did not work, had already driven away.

So they visited the bars. La Cigale first, but B.D. said the drinks were too expensive, and they left after one cognac. Then to the Farouk Bar and the Mona Lisa, where they had a beer apiece, until they came to the Gypsy Bar located among other bars with equally fanciful names on an obscure street in Da Kao. The front was shrouded with a grenade screen, and an old Viet in a soiled jacket which may at one time have been white got up jerkily from the corner where he had been squatting and opened the screen for them.

"What's that he's smoking?"

"Thuoc fin," B.D. said. "Marijuana to you. Grows wild. The Viets smoke it when they can't get opium."

They pushed through the door and stood in the entryway, heat flowing harshly around them like a river, though within the long, narrow room fans mounted on the ceiling danced in weird syncopation. A dim, smoke-layered room with shabby furniture, cheap plastic and faded upholstery brought from Japan or left by the French. A record player blasting shrill rock and the barman figuring a tab on blue lined graph paper. A few soldiers in fatigue uniforms and two others who could have been soldiers or anyone else talking to girls with short skirts slit up the leg and low bodices.

B.D. took a stool at the bar. The bartender put away his graph paper for a moment. "Ba-me-ba," B.D. said. "Unless you want something else."

"Beer's fine, but I can't take much more."

"You'll learn to like Vietnamese beer. That's all you can get upcountry."

Knox pointed to a sign behind the bar. "What are lady's dinks?"

27

"Ladies' drinks. The sign painter fucked up. Saigon tea to you. That's when you pay for tea when some broad asks you to talk to her. It's mostly leftover Coke. If she's going good a chick can pack away five or six in an hour, then give you the shaft if you try for a little nooky."

"Some life."

B.D. shrugged. "Anything to hustle a buck and put some chop in the bowl. They were probably happy before we came. I dunno, stands to reason they should have been, but you can't tell. Put somebody in paradise and pretty soon he'd be screwing up by the numbers."

One of the girls was at Knox's side now, rubbing her body slightly against him, swaying, touching. "Hey, GI, you buy me tea, talk maybe."

"No," Knox said.

"Fuck you, GI," the girl said. She flounced away.

B.D. laughed. "She's got spirit, that's what most Viets lack. Scratch most of them and I'll show you a rabbit." He ran his eye over another bargirl who was playing seven-card gin with the mama-san, her broad short face curling into slitted eyes and wide nostrils, and yet, like a caterpillar trying to shed its too tight skin, somehow delicately beautiful. "The world's most attractive women, or so some claim. You can't judge until you've had one."

"I'm sure Mister Balfour has explicit rules on the subject of fraternization."

"He's no prude. Just so happens he's got one of the nicest pieces of ass in Saigon tucked away."

"I'll pass on the local women."

"Got a wife waiting for you at home?"

"No, I guess not. What I mean to say is, we divorced. She got everything."

"They never get everything. You got the clothes you're standing in."

"She took everything else she could get."

"That's the screwing you get for the screwing you got."

"Thanks a lot," Knox said. And then, to change the subject: "Mister Balfour wasn't very specific about what I'll find at Phan Rang."

"Probably didn't want you wetting your pants."

"Bad up there?"

"It's no garden spot. You're taking the place of a man who went out today, only he was traveling in a box."

Knox rolled the beer glass between his palms. "Phan Rang sounds dangerous."

B.D. shrugged and gestured toward the bargirl who was playing seven-card gin with the mama-san. "Come here, honey, and tell old Bulldog your name."

The girl put down her cards and walked over gracefully. Her tight clothes made her breasts stand out prominently. "My name Rosette."

"Rosette, my associate here has had a trying day, maybe you can help him unwind."

Rosette put a hand on Knox's shoulder and reached up to loosen his tie. Knox drew back.

"I no hurt you."

B.D. laughed. He had a mouthful of beer and had to swallow it quickly. It left a foamy mustache on his upper lip. He pointed at Rosette's breasts. "That all Hong Kong."

Rosette stamped her foot and her breasts heaved. "That all me, no Hong Kong. No even te-te Hong Kong."

"Well give us a look."

"How much you pay?"

"Hell, Rosette, my associate's got the hots for you. Show him a little now and he'll make it worth your while." B.D. motioned to the barman and the barman slid another glass with a large piece of ice in it and another beer bottle across the counter.

Knox pointed to a number tattooed on the man's wrist. "What's that?"

"I dunno, it's got a French seven in it, but I've never seen any Viet with a tattoo like that."

Rosette snapped off the bottle cap with her teeth and poured the beer over the ice. "It French numba. French put on him long time. He took to France for carry big wagons."

B.D. grasped the bartender's wrist and looked closely at the number before the bartender jerked his arm away. "Yeah, I heard about that, read it somewhere maybe. The French impressed over half a million Viets as porters during the first big war. One out of every five or six died." He looked straight at the Vietnamese. "How long you have that, papa-san?"

The Viet shook his head. He pointed to B.D.'s glass. "You pay for dink."

"Sure, you don't want to talk about it. You know Ho chi Minh? He was in France about that time." B.D. put a hundred-piastre note on the counter. The bartender tried to pick it up but B.D. kept his hand on it. "Did you know Ho chi Minh when you were in France, old man?"

The bartender gave up trying to get the bill. "Never hear Ho chi Minh." He picked up his towel and moved away.

Rosette sidled closer to Knox. "You buy me tea for luckee."

"Khrist, who's this luckee I'm already hearing about?" B.D. swayed slightly on his barstool. "Every bar in town some chick comes up and wants a tea for luckee. Luckee's making out like a champ." B.D. finished his beer, reached over and patted Rosette on the fanny. She giggled and pushed his hand away.

"That's not Hong Kong, baby, that's the real stuff." He

slid to his feet. "Com'on, stud, you got a busy day tomor-row."

The bartender chattered something in the tonal Vietnam-ese that already Knox found annoying, mostly because he could not understand it. It was strange and therefore an-noying.

"What the hell does he want?"

"He wants you to pay the bill."

"I don't have any piastres, you know that."

"Don't worry, I've been keeping track of what you owe me." B.D. threw a five-hundred-piastre note on the bar. The Vietnamese sorted through the sodden bits of graph paper, pointing to the figures.

"You owe him 'nother hundret p," Rosette said.

B.D. dropped another five-hundred-piastre note on top of the first one. The bartender counted out one two-hundred and two one-hundred piastre notes. He dropped an MPC note, but quickly recovered it.

"Thanks, GI, you come back, see me, maybe."

"Maybe," said Knox.

"Don't count on it." B.D. lit another cigarette and started for the entrance. He stopped suddenly and thrust a one-hundred-piastre bill down the front of Rosette's sweater. "Maybe you remind the old man about Uncle Ho."

Rosette pulled out the wadded note, smoothed it and folded it leaflike around her fingers. "You come Gypsy Bar."

"Goddamn broad," B.D. said when they were outside.

Knox rattled some coins in his pocket.

"What's the matter, checking to see if you still got your nuts? Piss on it, you think this place was expensive, wait 'til you try Maxim's. You'll be lucky to get away with the skin on your dick." He waved hurriedly at a taxi going down a side street. The taxi stopped and turned around, lurching at them now, lights barely probing the still-enveloping, all-intense heat. "Got one first time. Sometimes you have to wave at four or five before one of our gallant allies will stop to take our money."

VI

They returned to B.D.'s villa, past the Cirque Sportif and all the sleeping houses, getting out of the taxi one block away and walking around the corner and down the short alley to the gate in the wall, then through that and into the courtyard behind the big house and the small villa where B.D. lived. The screen door was secured to a post with a heavy chain passed around the post and through a hole punched in the screen. A Vespa motorbike almost filled the small porch and they had to pass it single file. The Vespa was also chained to the post. B.D. fumbled at the lock in the darkness, then they were inside. He switched on the light and after a while the fluorescents came on. But they flickered intermittently because the current was low. A Sanyo table fan oscillated slowly on a table in the center of the room, so slowly that the individual plastic blades were visible through their transparent arcs of speed. B.D. jiggled the dials of a transformer but the lights did not brighten.

"May as well give up on it," Knox said.

B.D. did not reply. He opened the refrigerator door and took out a beer, stripping off the top and throwing it back into the refrigerator. "Help yourself. I don't charge extra for the beer. Long as you don't drink more than me."

Knox took off his shirt and sat down on the plastic-covered sofa. He misjudged the distance and sat down a little too hard. His mouth was dry for some reason. B.D. reached under the desk in the corner and pulled out a mildewed suitcase, scuffed and frayed. One strap was broken and the other had lost a buckle. He opened the lock with a small tool he had on his key chain. The light flickered out and B.D. cursed. The light came on. B.D.'s shirt was sodden except for the absolute tips of the collar. He moved the fan closer.

"Push me the trash can," he muttered. Knox saw only a cardboard carton. "The box, that one over there. Nothing fancy in my pad."

Knox pushed the box across the floor with his foot and B.D. threw the empty beer can into it. The can hit with a muffled clunk and the light went out again.

"Possumshit," B.D. said. "I wish I had stole some of those gas lanterns last time I was at Saigon Port." Then to Knox: "How about getting me another beer."

The fluorescent lights came on again with a snapping noise. Knox got a beer from the refrigerator and gave it to B.D., who stopped gnawing a fingernail long enough to take it. He flipped open the suitcase and immediately threw two shirts into the box.

"Those look like good shirts."

"You want them you can have them."

"Hell, I don't want them, but why throw them away?" Knox was overcautious because he was overcontrolled. He knew the joy of noncommitment.

"Because they belonged to Cresap, the troop from Phan Rang who got hisself killed. The people at the Air America office found it this afternoon. The Chief gave it to me to sort out."

"Did he stay with you when he came to Saigon?"

"Yeah, everybody stays with me when they come to Sai-

gon. You might even say Cresap and I were buddies. He
might not have got in such deep *nuoc mam* if he had called
me from the airport instead of trying to come in town alone.
I figured Charlie must have got him after he passed the QC
checkpoint down the road from the terminal. Whatever
info he had wouldn't have been of any value once they got
it out of him because they probably changed whatever it
was they had in mind as soon as he talked since they
thought he had got word to us anyhow."

"How're you so sure he talked?"

B.D. dropped a pair of trousers into the cardboard box
and picked up a packet of letters. He opened one and
scanned it hurriedly in the poor light. "Everybody talks in
this business. The Charlies don't have any of the exotics; no
time or technology. They just lop off the little finger to let
you know they mean business and then work up to the cord
around the skull until you tell them what it is they want to
know in the first place. They'll stomp the living piss out of
you and make you drink it. You only get killed when they
get tired."

Knox was perspiring heavily and he tasted the rubbery
salt of bile in his throat. He rubbed his palms surrepti-
tiously against his trousers.

B.D. tilted the beer can and drained it. "No more beer
for old Cresap. No more nooky. No more nothing."

"Anybody else at Phan Rang ever get hurt?"

"Best I can recall the office was mortared and one agent
got killed, but I was in Cambodge then. All the people
we've lost have been from upcountry." B.D. was slipping
the letters through his fingers into the box without the pretense of reading them.

"Aren't you going to send them back to his wife?"

"What for? She already knows what they say, and she
wouldn't want to know about those she didn't write."

"Oh."

"Yeah, oh." B.D. looked at the refrigerator and then at Knox. Knox got another can of beer from the refrigerator and threw it to B.D. B.D. tapped the top of the can with a pencil to settle the foam before opening it. He threw the rest of the letters into the trash box with a motion of disgust. He scratched his belly, then his crotch. "No good agent ever keeps letters, all sorts of possibilities for compromise. No wonder old Cresap got killed. Probably a good thing." The first to himself more than Knox. And then to Knox: "Why'd you come out here anyway?"

"My father thought it would be a good idea for me to get some experience in this sort of thing before going into the Foreign Service."

"Your father must have rocks in his head." Then again: "Of course it's better than being drafted. Going to follow in Daddy's footsteps, be the big ambassador someday."

"Perhaps. That's not impossible."

"Hardly likely either." B.D. resumed pawing through the suitcase. He came up with a cheap picture in a gold-colored frame, now tarnished. It had been wrapped in a shirt, but even so the glass had broken and cut into the picture of the woman it held. The pieces fell out as B.D. lifted it. He cut a finger on a sliver. "Sonabitch," he said, and sucked the finger.

"Looks like you're throwing out everything."

"Nothing his wife would want anyway. I think his old lady must have been something like yours. Cresap and his wife were on the edge of divorce a few times."

Knox shook his head. Even now, hearing the words, he could feel the old desolation, the old despair nudging a corner of his mind. The old self-pity and the old bitter consolations of that pity.

B.D. gathered up the trash box and poured the contents

back into the suitcase. He tore a strip from an undershirt and wrapped it around his cut finger.

"Just how did he die?" Knox finally asked the question. He had been waiting and wanting to ask it and he knew with a dreadful sort of certainty that B.D. had been waiting and wanting him to ask it, just as he was certain that B.D. wanted to answer it.

"Like no man should of. Even a dumb ass like Cresap. With his dick cut off and stuffed up his nose and his head sewed inside his belly with wire. They did other things to him, too. But they didn't whack off his peter until they got what they wanted. They never do that before you talk. Up 'til then you can always hope they're just playing."

Knox felt his crotch tingle. B.D. crushed the empty beer can between thumb and forefinger, then discarded it. "You can sleep in the bedroom. That's where I put your suitcases. I'll sleep out here."

Knox lay in the bed and the darkness, only the faintly cool humid air from the stir of the overhead fan covering him, throat dry from too much swallowing, and mouth with the sensation of lint. He heard a noise somewhere in the distance, far in the distance, and held his breath, blood pounding in his temples with a hollow, ringing sound as if his head were a cave as big as the dark outside. He got up and groped his way to the refrigerator, hoping to do so soundlessly, but bumping into things in his path, pausing after each small collision to wait breathlessly in the engloomed dark to hear if B.D. was awake and likewise listening.

He touched the refrigerator and found the handle, opening it and welcoming the shimmering glow of the small light like daybreak itself. The water was in a battered enamel pan and he did not see it for a time, looking instead for a jar or pitcher. In all his life he had never drunk from a pan and he spilled a lot of water down his chest until he learned not to tip it too high. Then the empty pan was inside the refrigerator and the light was gone and he groped back through the blackness, stubbing his toe painfully against the bed so that it shifted and the scraping reverberated through the villa, harsh and unreal in the quiet darkness, like a stone dropped in water and the ripples spreading out within his brain until he thought they would never stop. Wanting so hard he was sick from the wanting, but wanting so hard he had forgotten what he really wanted.

VII

The morning was the color of aluminum and Knox was talking to Mister Balfour again. He was sick from a cold which had started in the night. Knox felt light headed and weak, but he coughed a lot more than he had to. Mister Balfour turned and his glasses were once more like silver pennies in the light.

"So you think you like Saigon more than Phan Rang, is that it?"

Knox began with bland smoothness. "No, sir. I just thought about it a lot last night. I really don't know much about this business yet. The school doesn't prepare you for this kind of work. Not really. And I want to stay and learn as much as I can. Then when I'm ready to go upcountry I'll be a lot more valuable." He had a lot of experience in being smooth, and did not feel guilty about it anymore.

Mister Balfour nodded. "That's the heart of our troubles. We get too many inexperienced people out here. They come charging out full of piss and steam and next thing you know they're so screwed up they can't tell their ass from a hole in the ground. In a way it's refreshing to have somebody admit he doesn't know as much about this game as the Director." Mister Balfour drummed his fingers on the desk.

"What do you think?" Mister Balfour turned to B.D., who sat enveloped in his own cloud of cigarette smoke, saying nothing. Knox had forgotten he was in the room.

B.D. shrugged. "At least he's halfway honest. You've got more people coming in soon. One of them could just as easily go to Phan Rang. You're the Chief, you decide."

Knox sniffled. He was trying to be discreet now, but his eyes watered, then burned. "I'm not trying to get out of going to Phan Rang. I don't think I'm ready yet, that's the whole point. Give me a few months here and I'll be thinking like you do down here." He was arguing persuasively, logically, trying to keep the plea, the fear, from sounding in his voice. Hoping he would not have to use his most compelling argument, since he did not know if it really was an argument at all, or rather an invocation of something he did not even know was invocable.

B.D. began coughing. Great, wheezing coughs that doubled him up in his chair. At length he stopped and sat up again. He reached for a cigarette in his shirt pocket.

"Those cigarettes are going to kill you." Mister Balfour leaned back in his chair and made a pyramid with his fingers. "Haven't you been reading in the papers about the connection between cancer and smoking?"

"Anyone can stop smoking," B.D. said, his voice weak, breathless. "It takes guts to face cancer."

Mister Balfour turned back to Knox. "Medical facilities at Phan Rang are primitive. The Air Force has a dispensary at the field, but I don't know how good their treatment is. I wouldn't want that cold to develop into something else. For the sake of your father and your own career with the Agency I'm going to leave you here for the time being. You'll have the opportunity to learn CAS from the ground up. The right way. I'll still use you to run some liaison missions upcountry. The Phoenix type especially. Then when I think you have enough experience you'll go up to one of the detachments."

"Thank you," Knox said, keeping the relief, the success, from showing in his voice. Mister Balfour had invoked the invocable, but he still did not know if that had been the persuasive argument.

"You make good out here and you can write your own ticket. Everybody from Mr. Helms on down is watching this operation closely. We can't afford to send out less than our best, no matter how long it takes." Mister Balfour's lips closed into the straight line of a well-healed surgical scar.

"Yes, sir, I'll learn all I can." He knew he would have no trouble remaining in Saigon. For he knew how not to make influential enemies. He was good at flattery, had a passion for conformity. He made enemies, but he selected them carefully. Knox did not want Mister Balfour as an enemy.

B.D. caught up with him in the hallway. The Vietnamese, Mr. Khiem, was not in his office. "You have perfect diction," B.D. said. "And that sounds intelligent and fools people. Your voice is so mellifluous that when you say something people believe you."

"I don't understand."

"You understand. That was a good con job. You're going to have to find another place to stay. By next week. That's the most I can give you."

And so Knox came to learn the basics of the craft of intelligence. The everyday nitty-gritty not mentioned in the school. The morass of undigested intelligence which poured in, the information sold to more than one source, each agency in the sprawling tangle of governmental intelligence establishments wanting to outdo the other, each regarding itself as the one true guardian of integrity in the process of gathering information. Information which the agencies wanted to hear, not necessarily that which actually *is*. Documents moving with elephantine lugubriousness, data which was impossible to collate or cross-check. The various symbols of evaluation, the grinding sameness of allusions, probabilities, assumptions and unwillingness of anyone to commit himself; seeking refuge in the numbers and the letters which allegedly explained it all, but which really explained nothing. In short, Knox was beginning to see what it was like to be an agent.

VIII

He found himself returning to the Gypsy Bar. Not going there directly, but walking there sometime late in the afternoon of his third day in Saigon. Walking because he was as yet uncertain the taxis were safe, and with his money not changed to scrip. In the late afternoon with the sunlight less harsh now, though just as sourceless as always. Through the downtown section, past combat veterans on the streets, young men with old hard eyes screwed into once soft faces. Young troops riding Hondas and Suzukis, unwashed fatigues open and snapping behind, gunning their engines for the sound and the exhilaration of it; beeping their horns, causing old men and young children to quicken their steps when crossing streets. "Hey, GI, you want boom-boom," shouted by a street urchin as he made a graphic and quite obscene gesture.

He entered the Gypsy Bar and found no customers there yet, only the bartender with the tattoo on his wrist, the mama-san and the bargirl — Rosette. The fans were not on and the room was oppressively hot. But as he sat down the mama-san touched a switch and the fans began to revolve. Rosette sat beside him. The bartender placed a tea and a bottle of Bier 33 with ice in a glass on the counter. Rosette snapped off the cap with her teeth, then poured the beer into the glass down the side so it did not foam. Knox took a sip, and discovered thirst, drinking noisily now, the astringent taste of the preservative burning in his throat. When he put it down the glass was empty and flocked with the drying foam and inner chill.

"Let me take you to dinner."

Rosette shook her head and he caught the sour-woman smell, the staleness of woman flesh cheaply perfumed. "No can do, GI. Mama-san no let me. Less you pay. Then maybe she let me go, three, maybe fo' hour. All night you pay enough."

"What does the mama-san have to do with whether you have dinner with me or not?"

"No stay work she fire me, no get bar work any bar else."

Soldiers in camouflage fatigues and unit patches came in and took stools at the end of the bar. Bargirls, their hair slick with oil, as brightly clothed as butterflies, moved surely, confidently toward the soldiers. One of them pinched a bargirl and they all laughed. The soldiers ordered drinks and made room for the girls to sit with them.

"What the hell, mama-san doesn't own you."

Rosette shrugged and drank all of her tea. The bartender paused in his trips to the other end of the bar and poured Rosette another tea. The all-seeing mama-san scratched another mark on the slip of graph paper which served as Rosette's tally.

"Well, what if I pay mama-san what you make in a night, then could I take you to dinner?" Knox wondered why he had asked in the first place. It had been an impulsive thing to do. Perhaps because he had been denied the right to make decisions of importance and therefore wanted to make decisions he could regard as important.

Rosette slipped off her barstool and went around to the mama-san. She whispered to the mama-san and the mama-san whispered back, and Rosette returned and told Knox: "Two thousand dong."

"How much is that?"

"Almost twenty dollar. She say take MPC or dong, either you want to pay."

"That's a lot of money just to take you to dinner. You should be paying me."

"You no want take me okay. You take, you pay two thousand dong," Rosette said firmly.

"Okay, okay, I want to take you to dinner tomorrow."

The soldiers at the end of the bar were drunk. Eyes unnaturally bright, voices shrill. Drinking heavily because they did not have the slightest idea of what they were doing or interest in it, nor had they any hope for the future or even an understanding of it. For they, like Knox, did not believe in their own destiny.

"I'm going to be in Saigon for a time, maybe you can help me find a place to live."

"Upstairs for rent."

Knox shook his head. "Too much noise. I want a house somewhere it's quiet."

The bartender brought Knox another beer. The beer he had already drunk was acid in his stomach. "Then I meet you here tomorrow night. Six-thirty. You look for me a house, okay?"

Rosette nodded sagely and sipped another tea. "Okay, GI, you, me for eat."

"Six-thirty then." His stomach was queasy and Knox turned to go. The bartender shouted something and threw some wet squares of graph paper on the bar. The tattoo left from the time he had been a porter or a PIM moved in and out of the light.

"You no pay," Rosette said.

Knox took out his wallet. He saw the green currency. He had been eating with B.D. and had not yet converted his money to scrip or bought piastres. "I'll have to pay him tomorrow."

The bartender was peering anxiously over the counter. He saw the folds of bills in the wallet and peered closer. Rosette whistled. The bartender grabbed her arm and whispered something urgently in her ear.

"He say he take that for pay. Maybe you buy dong from him with that monies."

"All right, what's it going to cost if I pay with this?"

Rosette translated and the bartender calculated quickly. "He say five dollar enough. If you want buy piastres he give you good trade. He sell MPC too."

Knox shrugged. "All right. How much can he give me for what I have here?"

"How much you have?"

Knox started to count it onto the bar but the Vietnamese bartender stopped him and hurried him to a table where he sat down with his back blocking the soldiers from seeing them. Knox counted the bills onto the wet tabletop. He had $310. The bartender wrote something on a scrap of paper and showed it to Rosette.

"He say you get four hundret dollar fifty MPC for money you have." Then in a lower voice, "Ask five hundret, he give you."

Knox said "Five hundred" very slowly and distinctly, spreading the fingers of one hand. The bartender nodded reluctantly. He gathered up the bills and started to leave. Knox stopped him and took the money. The bartender grinned.

Rosette leaned over. "Next time you have money bring here. He give you numba one price."

The bartender came back and sat down in the same position as before, then counted out five hundred dollars in the orange-brown ten-dollar MPC notes.

"See you tomorrow, GI." Rosette waved good-bye and he pushed through the door and out into the night warm as new milk. He felt braver and hailed a taxi, even giving the address properly and paying the driver off in scrip and getting nine dollars in MPC change. He was learning to get around in Saigon.

IX

So he bought her freedom, at least for the evening, and took his time doing what he had planned all along. First they had dinner at the Quilliam Tell, riding through Cholon streets darkened by a power failure, people like wraiths, unseen except in the dim, puny glow of headlights or kerosene lanterns hung inside stores. To the Quilliam Tell and dinner there. Alone and isolated with each other by the illumination of two candles stuck pseudo-Italianate in necks of empty bottles. With the waiters in spotted, stained white jackets passing among them amid the clink of dinnerware and every now and again the muttered concussion of an artillery shell faint in the distance. Waiters with mediocre English and equivalent service apprehensive in the shadows, but no one took any notice or even looked up.

For this was customary, and they had long ago absorbed the sounds of shellfire into subconsciousness.

They had two beef dinners with French fries and a bottle of Algerian wine from which Rosette drank little, leaving most of her glass untouched throughout the awkward dinner. The bottle of wine was wet from melted ice, and after a while the label slid off to reveal that it was really a Korean beer bottle. Knox addressed himself to his food. The meat was tough, stringy, and the potatoes were greasy. So Knox drank the entire bottle of wine, giving up after a few more desultory attempts to talk with Rosette.

He took his time, eating everything put before him, relishing Rosette's discomfort. He had a cup of the strong French coffee, using his fingers to put in large broken lumps of raw sugar until the bitterness was lost in the cloying sweetness of half a cup of undissolved sugar. At least it helped the first faint flashes of drunkenness to pass and he could see more clearly now, though he was immoderately proud he had drunk all the wine, even finishing the half-glass Rosette had left while he waited for the check.

It was expensive. He already knew that; yet he was curiously loath to part with so much money in piastres. The sum of the blue bills bulked enormously in his mind and on the waiter's tray. So huge that he took everything, even the small piastre coins with the serrated edges, the waiter brought back as change, then unceremoniously pushed Rosette ahead of him out the door and into the darkened street still corpulent with heat. They passed several pedicabs and their drivers called out but he ignored them, standing at the buckled stone curbing, Rosette small and defensive beside him; waiting in the dark, the swelter of things unseen and tangible smells, for a taxi to pass, but none stopped.

So he finally settled for a motorized junk. Wedging himself and Rosette into the worn metal basket of the cyclo with its slab cushions which offered little protection from the jolts. Giving the driver the address by the name of the street, Hong thap Tu, and riding with Rosette taut beside him down the dips and sways of road.

When they passed the intersection of Le van Duyet with Hong thap Tu Knox waved the junk to the side. They got out and he gave the cyclo driver fifty piastres but the driver demanded more, one hundred piastres, shouting, "Hondret p, hondret p." Knox was almost ready to give him another fifty piastres when Rosette grasped him by the arm and they walked away, she leading him and the click, scrape of her high heels sharp, bright sounds in the night. The cyclo driver yelled something and drove in their direction, one wheel in the street and the other wheel on the sidewalk. He spat at Knox as he passed.

"This good place," Rosette said from ahead of him. "Westmoreland live not much far from this. Many Canh Sat patrol, keep you okay."

"Yes," he said in a dry furious voice, "I stay very safe." He had a hand on her waist and excitement was rising. He was clumsy in opening the doors. The electricity was off here and he struck two matches before he could light the kerosene lamp.

Knox turned up the wick and her face came out of the dark into the small, pitiful flare of lamplight. He shut the door and the room was close and airless. Rosette sat on the sofa, her eyes dilated in the dimness, standing out like opals in the shadows of her face. Knox crossed over to where she sat and lifted her chin, seeing the miniature beads of clear perspiration caught in the faint down of her upper lip, the quick flick of her tongue through parted teeth, smelled again the sour, stale woman flesh.

"You have tea for me, GI, then you me Gypsy Bar take."

"Later," Knox said, and very deliberately he brought his face down upon hers and kissed her. She drew away.

"You no nice, GI," she said, pouting.

"Why you think I brought you here?" Knox snapped.

Rosette hesitated, confused. "Me no sure. No GI ever pay price to take me for dinner before."

Knox tried to kiss her again. She pushed him away. He

was aware of his penis springing hot and cobralike from between his loins. He sat beside her and she was at the end of the sofa, could go no further. He seized her shoulders and kissed her forcibly, filling her mouth with his, stilling her cries, and then with one hand ripping open her blouse, pulling down her thin brassiere, seizing a breast and massaging the nipple into erectness.

She scratched his face, frantically, furiously, the clawing half-pain, half-pleasure to him now. Knox seized her hands and pinioned them both. They were both breathing heavily. The sound of it filled the room with a strange rasping. He stopped kissing her long enough to blow gently into her ear. She reacted violently. He moved his thighs hard against hers and the tempo of her breathing changed, though she still struggled. She was no match for him.

With his right hand Knox freed her of her shirt and then unzipped his trousers, falling to his knees on the floor as he kissed her lower down, then rising to cover her, pressing her between himself and the hot plastic sofa, writhing against her with slow, harsh sweeps. Bruising and thrusting, forcing himself deeper so that she groaned, leaning his full weight against her and feeling the surprise of a hymen. She bit his lower lip and Knox tasted the saltiness of his own blood. Part of the blood and saliva slipped out and traced down her chin to mingle with the sweat standing in the fold of her neck.

His undershorts held his legs, and he kicked one leg free, clamping his legs around her knees, thinking now of a rubber, but knowing it was too late. They broke apart. Her clothes crushed and covered here and there with body stains. Two people closely bound together still on a tiny sweat-covered plastic couch at the bottom of a tight, airless room. In the dim glow of the kerosene lamp Knox could see tears pooled at the corners of her eyes.

Rosette struggled against him and this time he let her have her way. She smoothed down her skirt, then pulled her blouse over her shoulders and looked away. "You buy new dress, you mess this."

Knox did not answer. He thought he heard a footstep on the porch. But B.D. was not coming home this night, had gone to Vung Tau as a courier. The webbing of the couch creaked as she slowly turned, then leaned sideways to kiss him gently on the temple.

"You love me, GI?"

"Sure I love you, Rosette."

"You beaucoup sou me, GI." But she giggled and kissed him again. He was conscious of the heat which threatened to stifle him. "You take me home, GI."

"It's late, Rosette, I have to work early tomorrow."

She laughed. "You funny, GI. You boom-boom me first time and you no even want take me home." Rosette got up and took the lamp. She walked to the rear of the villa and he heard the bathroom door close. After a while the toilet flushed and he sat there alone in the darkness with the heat and her musky woman smell rank in his nostrils. She came back and he was on his feet as she brought her own small cocoon of light until they both stood in it. "You come see me tomorrow, GI?"

He did not answer but pressed some piastre notes into her free hand. She looked at the bills, then handed them back except for one fifty-piastre note.

"Taxi not cost me much. Buy me tea later, yes?" She did not try to kiss him as she passed, only brushed his arm lightly with her fingers. She left the lamp on the table by the door and closed it ever so quietly. He took the lamp to find his way to bed.

X

Rosette found him a house on Tran cao Van Street, not very far from the site on Thong Nhut where the new American Embassy was being built. It was a small villa which had once been servants' quarters behind the larger house of the owner. It was similar to B.D.'s except that it was not enclosed within the main courtyard but was outside, and was reached by going down a narrow alley between high walls which opened into its own small courtyard. It was also reached by a gate cut in the wall if Knox did not use the alley. Sometimes the owner parked his old black Renault in the alleyway, and unless it was parked very close against one wall Knox had to go through the main courtyard and the gate. But he did not mind, for the car effectively blocked the alley and made a good grenade screen.

He paid a good price for it, too, even signing a lease for a lower price than he was really paying, the owner looking at him slyly as he signed the faint blue graph paper. He did not even ask Rosette how she had found it, for already he knew that she had her ways. He paid twenty-five thousand piastres a month instead of the fourteen thousand the lease specified, and the landlord said he would install an air conditioner. And when it was installed the USAID shield with the brown and white hands clasping had been painted over, though Knox could still see the outline of the shield dimly through the hastily applied paint.

There was an aquarium in the living room, something stored there by the owner. A two-hundred-liter glass-sided tank with the caulked seams dry but still serviceable. Rosette brought him some fish. They were small and delicate, with long, lacy fans for tails and sleek torpedo shapes, graceful in every movement. He was to spoil all that when he unknowingly put in a Siamese fighting fish he brought home in a glass fruit jar from the fish market. That was all to come later, after he had discovered the tropical fish market and the bull-necked fighting fish with the iridescent colors and ethereal fins and the little boys who sold fish from plastic bags held hooplike on concentric rings of wire growing like a Christmas tree from the fender of a bicycle's rear wheel. But he did not discover the savage viciousness of the fighting fish until afterward, and then of course it was too late. All he had left was the one fighting fish until Rosette brought him some more fish and changed the water; and, when he was not looking, threw the fighting fish into the yard to let it die.

Knox had three rooms, a large living room with the usual cheap plastic sofa and a table with chairs already warp-legged past all hope of ever sitting evenly, a screen that hid the rusty refrigerator and the alcove which served as a kitchen with the two-burner gas stove he would hardly ever use and one small iron skillet. Two more rooms, one for a bedroom with a sparse wooden frame for the bed and foam rubber for a mattress; the other he would never use except for the people he would meet who would stay there because it had a bed and a toilet, too, even though the chain on the water closet had rusted through and been repaired with a length of plastic piping.

Knox was the prince and possessor of this empire, to include the portable Sanyo radio and the aquarium, for as long as he paid the rent of twenty-five thousand piastres a month, or, in terms he could more easily grasp, $213 at the official rate.

He lived there and liked it after a fashion, because he had to share it with no one, except Rosette, unless he wanted to; and no one from the office ever came to know where he actually lived, even though he conscientiously entered the address in the duty agent log. He did not have a telephone. Telephones were luxuries you learned to live without, and that was just as well considering the phone system. He did have the uncomfortable feeling that B.D. knew where he lived and what he was doing.

The office was close enough to walk to, but he tried to be mysterious. Knox left and returned at odd hours, and went by various routes. Sometimes he would go around by the Basilica or the back streets by the Botanical Gardens. There he would see urchins on rooftops flying small kites made from newspaper with long fierce tails, held captive against the incessant lure of the wind by incredibly long thin threads wound around San Miguel beer bottles.

And Rosette would be there. Only infrequently at first, then more often, and discreetly, for he had a cleaning woman who came every morning except Sundays for one thousand piastres a month and did a reasonably good job of keeping the villa clean. To avoid the talk he thought would follow disclosure he kept Rosette hidden, apart in her own separate cubicle of the life he was neatly ordering. Making for himself a secure little island in the midst of time.

He took her to bed, for she was like all women, and women were like water, molding to whatever they touched. Clinging, receding, tepid, yet able to wear away stone. He discovered pleasure again. Or pleasure discovered him. Pursued or pursuer, the end was the same. Making love to her with energy and determination. On the foam rubber mattress with the air conditioner making the sheets silky cool and luxuriant. Mounting her in all the standard configurations because these were what he had learned or heard about. She responded, but after a while it was forced. They both knew it, though he wished it could be as natural as a season coming, or a flower blossoming. Any of the things which were natural. Still, at that point in time and infinity everything in him focused on the point of flooded cavernosa for one sweet, agonizing half-minute until he felt himself go flaccid. Yet this too was natural, for Knox wanted all good times preserved in amber and the bad experiences buried in quicklime. Already he had forgotten about his wife, the divorce. Perhaps it had never happened.

Though once he thought about his wife, only once. When Rosette had done something which reminded him very much of her. And he lay in the cool, rumpled sheets afterward with the dissatisfaction like lemon juice. Something, a vague unease. "Because you are and I am," she had said. "It's an arrangement founded on the very nature of things, and that's cause enough." Though he had never thought about the words long enough before to really understand them or let them bother him. And he did not let them bother him now. They were all hiding from something; the difference was whatever it was they were hiding from.

Inevitably Knox talked. He casually dropped such cryptic abbreviations as KGB, M16, SDECE, OSI, NISO, and did not bother to even try to explain them because Rosette would not have understood anyway. It was enough to know that she was wide eyed at the casual mention of any initials. They maintained their surreptitious liaison and farcical circuitousness, all the while talking as if the successful prosecution of the war was contingent upon his labors. And Rosette, duly impressed by the fact he had money and apparent position, gave more than credence to the strange obtuseness of his behavior, and was misled by her own cupidity and simple intrigue.

Once Knox looked into the back room of a meat shop as he passed, his gaze caught by the roasted pigs' heads burned red with crisp ears scorched to cinders ready to crinkle at the slightest touch, and thought he saw through momentarily parted bead curtains a picture of Ho chi Minh. When he casually mentioned this to another agent, he seriously suggested they write an IIR on it because they had not made their quota that month and reports were slow in coming from the upcountry detachments; and they wanted to have enough figures to fit in the neat blocks for the monthly summary someone so laboriously prepared and everyone else so laboriously ignored. But they could not decide how to do it properly, and after a long discussion they regretfully gave it up. Though afterward Knox went through the other agents' desks late at night, searching for unfinished notes on the theory that stealing from one was plagiarism, but quoting two or more was research.

Thu Dien Vien
(The Pleasures of the Country Life)

I

"I WANT YOU to take the train," Mister Balfour said. "I want a report on track conditions. Some reports indicate the line is open. Some say it's not. Some say it's open only in certain places. You ride the train to Da Lat. Fly back. Let me know the condition of the trackage. I want a report, an immediate report, on how it goes. That was in our agreement, wasn't it?"

"Yes, that was our agreement."

"Okay, then. You'll be going up to Phan Rang by yourself. One of the agents at Phan Rang will meet you at the train station and go with you to Da Lat. He's a real fine agent, been in and out of Indochina half his life. Knew Ho chi Minh when Ho worked for the OSS. He's going up to interrogate any prisoners taken during this particular Phoenix."

Knox said nothing. Privately he wondered why Mister Balfour did not have a plane fly along the track. That seemed to him the best way to determine the track conditions.

"You're probably wondering why I don't just send a plane from here to there, have it fly above the track. Isn't that what you're thinking?"

Knox still said nothing. He knew Mister Balfour would answer the question for him.

"Because a strip of film doesn't tell me what the people are doing, what they're saying, what they're thinking. It can't show likely ambush spots or weak rails with the accuracy of an on-the-spot observer. That's why." Mister Balfour tossed a pencil into a half-open drawer. "You'll have a week to write up your observations after you return. But I'll want to hear about the Phoenix Operation as soon as you're back."

Knox blinked his eyes. Mister Balfour bent over some papers. Knox let himself out the door. He found B.D. in his tiny cubby of an office.

"You're going to Da Lat with Fumarole."

"Who's Fumarole?"

"He's an agent at CAS, Phan Rang. Bills himself as an old Asia hand. Once met Uncle Ho when Ho was rescuing downed fliers as a sideline. Turned the fliers over to the old OSS and got some guns and money from them. Fumarole's been talking about that ever since."

"I guess I'm going."

"No guessing about it. Your boarding passes and cover are on your desk. Take a camera along. You're supposed to be a stringer or something like that."

"Should I take a gun?"

"Up to you. You'll probably pick one up at Da Lat. But don't burden yourself with one between here and there unless you can use it. When you get to Phan Rang ask Fumarole for some of his Chieu Hoi passes."

"What are they?"

"Chieu Hoi means 'open arms.' People who are thinking about rallying to the South Viets turn themselves in with them. The psywar troops drop them by the millions over VC territory. Supposedly no one loyal to the government would have one. If you shoot a Vietnamese just stuff a few Chieu

Hoi passes in his pocket. Makes him a automatic Cong. You just happened to shoot him before he could rally."

"What's my cover again?"

"You're a reporter, not first-line or anything like that, just a stringer."

"I got that part, who am I supposed to be working for?"

"Hell, the MACV press card doesn't say who you work for, just pick a name. One is as good as another. There're more reporters out here than soldiers."

So Knox took his press credentials and went. Taking a taxi to the train station in Cholon and after a long wait finally rattling out of the station in a boxcar filled with *nha ques*, pigs, crated chickens, some US Army B-rations and two Popular Forces troops sitting behind a lightly sandbagged emplacement in the boxcar door with a rusty machine gun pointed aimlessly through the opening. The train rattled over the Bien Hoa Bridge and Knox saw flashes of the Saigon River through the door — brown, with the dull sheen of a rubber band. He slept while the train rumbled through the coastal towns, then roughly paralleled Rue Nationale One. Dozing fitfully in his cramped position against the wall, uncomfortable in the brooding heat.

There were a lot of delays and it took the train the better part of eighteen hours to cover the two hundred odd kilometers to Phan Rang. One of the *nha ques* broke into the B-rations when the two Popular Forces guards were asleep and passed out surreptitious cans to the other people in the car, then opened them with the small folding GI can openers they all seemed to have, one finding the large olive-drab can of bacon and eating it raw, his neighbors moving over to dip their hands into the can and fish out strips of the greasy bacon, not talking because of the guards. But then one of the guards awakened. He woke his fellow and the *nha ques* stopped eating for a moment, until the guards joined them in rifling the ration boxes of spam and eggs, the crackers and the canned bread. They ignored Knox and he was able to stretch his legs finally because the *nha que* in front of him had taken a can of chicken and was squatting by the sandbags. Every now and again one of the Vietnamese would toss an empty can from the boxcar and forage in the ration boxes for something else. They were all talking now, passing cans from one to the other. A Vietnamese pulled a canister of black pepper from the ration boxes. It was the last item. He heaved the empty ration box through the door and the toothless old woman on Knox's left cackled with delight. Someone had given her a small can of pasteurized cheese spread and she was dipping it out with a chopstick.

The Vietnamese with the can of pepper had it taken away from him by the biggest *nha que*. There was a brief scuffle but the big *nha que* won possession of the can. He squatted while he patiently opened the bottom of the can and pried back the thin flap of metal. He was disappointed with the contents and stirred the pepper tentatively with his forefinger. Then he tipped his head back and opened his mouth, tilting the can until a stream of pepper poured over the lip of the can and into his mouth. He swallowed once. Automatically. Then he screamed and hurled the can away. The contents spilled throughout the boxcar and the Vietnamese began sneezing. Knox watched in fascination as the *nha que* who had swallowed the pepper sprang about the car, throat working, but no sound coming out, tears swelling in great buds from the corners of his eyes, hands grasping his throat as he stumbled over other Vietnamese. Finally he found his voice and began crying. The old woman beside Knox gave the man a gourd filled with *nuoc mam* and he drank it. All of it. The *nha que* shuddered after he had drunk it, then went to the corner of the boxcar which the Vietnamese had selected as the latrine and puked. Knox put his head on his arms and slept.

The monotony of the ride was broken only by stops at villages to unload something, usually livestock, and take on more passengers. Their progress was minute and the stops long. The train passed through a Chan village and some Chans got in the boxcar. They sat in one corner all to themselves; they were still untouched, still unassimilated into Vietnamese culture after five hundred years. The boxcar filled with people so that Knox could hardly move. Which was fortunate because someone tried to steal his camera. He was able to get it back before the thief had gone very far. Knox was glad he recovered the camera. He was signed for it. Otherwise he would not have worried too much.

II

A man in sand-colored Saigon fatigues was waiting for him on the station platform. "I've been waiting for you hours, old man, couldn't you hurry that fucking train?"

"I was just along for the ride."

"I hope you got plenty of rest. The train to Da Lat is just ready to leave now. We haven't any time."

"Have we got to leave right away? I'm dead tired."

"That's rummy, old sport, but we've got an operation to see about and this is the only train. I'm Henry Fumarole. Call me Hank or Fumarole, whichever pleases you. Is that your bag?"

"Yes."

"You don't believe in traveling light, I must say. Well, let's press on with it. The train to Da Lat won't wait." Fumarole took Knox's suitcase, which was showing a lot of scuff marks now, and led the way across the rotting platform to another train. Some of the Vietnamese waiting on the platform looked at them triumphantly as they passed. Knox limped slightly because one leg was asleep.

The train to Da Lat was a convertible cog German engine scaling with rust and blisters of old paint. Two flatcars loaded with rocks and dirt were coupled ahead of the engine.

A Vietnamese in ragged sweater got up from his squatting position in the fitful shade of the tin roof and handed Fumarole a Chinese-made AK-47 assault rifle and a kit bag. The neck of a bottle of Johnny Walker protruded from the flap of the kit bag. Fumarole tossed the Vietnamese two large brass keys and the Vietnamese shuffled off. "My houseboy," Fumarole said. "A good-for-nothing buggar, but he knows his way around Phan Rang and he's honest as Viets go. That's really saying something when you're talking about a Viet."

"Didn't he have a number tattooed on his arm?"

"Noticed that, did you? Yes. He was a PIM. Lots of them around. He's an active TB case. Had it ever since the French pressed him. Wonder he's lived so long." Fumarole pulled himself into a baggage car.

"Isn't there a passenger car on this damn train either? I'm tired of riding in boxcars."

"You're out of luck, old man. Hasn't been a passenger car on this run for three years. That's how long ago the last passenger train was blown up. Saigon never got around to sending up any more passenger cars. Maybe they don't have any more." A Vietnamese youth came up and held out his hand. Fumarole gave him his boarding pass. He told Knox to do the same. The boy gave the passes to an elderly Vietnamese in a white pith helmet. Seeing they were looking at him the old Vietnamese shook his head gravely. "That's the stationmaster," Fumarole said. "He tries to discourage Americans from riding the train. Says it makes more of a target that way." He laughed and waved at the stationmaster. The stationmaster looked away.

There was a blast of discordant sound from the train's whistle. Three Popular Forces soldiers drinking beer under a poncho stretched against the station wall dropped their bottles and ran toward the baggage car. Two of them lifted a Honda into the door. They grinned at Knox. He grinned back. "You no be afraid. We keep you from VC."

"That's great to hear," Knox said. The third Popular Forces soldier was handing in a decrepit bicycle and three M-1 carbines.

"Yeah, great," Fumarole said, "we're being protected by the pig fuckers."

Knox hung the camera strap over a nail driven into the side of the baggage car. He looked around for a clean place to sit but found none, so he sat on his suitcase. The train began to move in jerks. One of the PF soldiers dangled his feet out the door. Fumarole offered the man a cigarette. The Vietnamese took it. "Fank you," he said.

"Up yours, Jack, and don't mention it." Fumarole frowned at the sky. "Looks like rain in the mountains." He took a pull at his bottle. He did not offer it to Knox.

"You got a raincoat?"

"No, we're in a baggage car, aren't we?"

"You don't know Vietnamese baggage cars."

They were moving out of the three-sided shed now, rumbling on the twin rusted bars of iron that served for track. They were suddenly swallowed up in the greenness of the jungle. Without warning they quit the sand and red dust and jerry-built shanties beside the tracks, and the sound of the engine, vastly muffled by the jungle, was all they heard.

After a while the train climbed out of the jungle and stopped at a village in low sandhills which Fumarole said was Da Tho. A Vietnamese Army aspirant in a plastic raincoat got aboard. He did not speak to them. Knox got out of the baggage car and stood on the muddy ground beside the ballast. The rain which had begun half an hour ago had not slackened and his throat was tight from new cold. He got between two cars and pissed. He felt better than he had in a long time. Some freight was unloaded and a wicker basket of angry geese was placed in the engineer's compartment. The only impression he carried away of Da Tho was fog and mud. Twenty minutes later they switched to cog track.

Fumarole screwed the cap back on his bottle and returned it to his kit bag. It was raining harder now. The drum of the rain intensifying until it blotted out the sound of the engine. The roof began to leak and Fumarole pulled out a poncho. Rain pelted off him in a fine mist. Water ran into Knox's eyes and he had difficulty seeing. "You should always carry a rain-coat in that nice roomy suitcase of yours." Then again a little later: "You want under a piece of this poncho?"

Knox shook his head.

"Suit yourself."

One of the PF soldiers lay down on a soggy mattress in a show of disregard for the rain. Knox was thoroughly chilled and began coughing. He tucked his hands under his armpits. The rain fell in a steady rhythm, and he was nodding despite the chill and the rain.

He was startled by gunfire at close range. Fumarole had gone to sleep but he had his AK-47 out now and pointed toward the door. Warily. Eyes suddenly awake and narrowed like a leopard's. One of the PF soldiers smiled and gave the thumbs-up sign. He was the one who had taken Fumarole's cigarette. His companion at the door triggered off another burst of carbine fire into the pines creeping slowly by in the fog. "We shoot. VC hear us and be afraid." The other PF had not moved from his ragged mattress. The aspirant was eating rice from a bowl by molding the rice into balls with his fingers.

"You know why they call them pig fuckers now." Fumarole gave the PF soldiers a cigarette each. He settled back and shook the water out of his eyes. "This looks a lot like the country around Kumming where I first met Ho."

"I was told that you knew Ho."

Fumarole had his bottle out again. "Past tense is correct. He brought a flier out of the jungle and one of the intelligence types thought he might be useful in gathering low-grade information. Funny thing, he refused a reward at first. We finially gave him some pistols and a picture of Chennault. He really must have impressed the other Indochinese working with him."

"Sounds like he was using American aid to build up his support."

"Stranger things than that have happened."

"What was he really doing for us?"

"Just what I said. Gathering low-level intelligence and every now and again bringing in some poor bastard who ran out of ideas and altitude simultaneously. Such things as how many Japs were operating in a given area, health of the population, Jap morale, weather, agriculture trends, that sort of thing."

"How good was he?"

"No better, no worse than the rest of the slopes working for us." Fumarole spoke casually. "Sometimes I think the wheels at Headquarters keep me around just because I once knew Ho. There aren't many Americans who can say that. Not live ones anyway. Sort of a prestige thing to have me around and trot me out occasionally to impress some dignitary."

"I'm sure that's not the reason."

"I'm sure it is. Why keep me around otherwise?" The rain was letting up now and Fumarole had propped up a corner of his poncho with the barrel of the AK-47. The bottle was already half-empty.

The train trembled to a sudden stop and Knox fell to the floor. The side of his shirt was smeared with mud when he regained his balance. The PF soldiers in the doorway swayed unsteadily. One fired his carbine at nothing in particular until the magazine was empty. Fumarole put up a hand to shield himself from the ejected cartridge cases.

Knox's ears were ringing from the noise in the closed space. The aspirant crawled across the floor of the baggage car and cautiously peered around the edge of the door. After a moment he stood up and jumped out, as agile as a cat. Fumarole followed him.

"Why don't you wait," Knox said. "It may be a trap."

"Baby, it sure as hell isn't a trap when an ARVN leaves cover in broad daylight and heads toward it."

So Knox followed. He sloshed through mud and ballast rocks to the locomotive. A massive pine felled either by accident or design lay across the tracks; the cowcatcher almost nuzzled it.

"VC blockade?"

"No." Fumarole pointed to the tangle of roots, then to a hole in the sandy hillside. "Hardly likely. Not unless they've got a few fellows the size of Steve Reeves."

Knox started to say something.

"Forget it," Fumarole said.

The aspirant was shouting instructions at the PF soldiers. One of them scurried back to the baggage car and returned with a machete. The brakeman handed another soldier a small hatchet with gaps in the cutting edge. It and the machete were equally dull. The soldiers began alternately to hack at the tree and stop to debate the futility of their task. Fumarole sat down on the cowcatcher. The aspirant was haranguing the soldiers. The train crew busied themselves lighting American cigarettes. Finally the trainmaster hurried up under the weight of a length of rusty chain. He looped the chain around the trunk and attached the other end to the cowcatcher. The engineer reversed the train and slowly slipped the pine off the track. The soldiers clapped their hands politely. The aspirant glared at them; then hastily ducked as the chain snapped and the end, taunt with strain, whipped over his head to smash against the locomotive with a high, singing sound.

"Let's get the fucking show on the fucking road," Fumarole said. Knox said nothing. They got back in the baggage car and the train inched forward again. They climbed a low grade and through breaks in the fog Knox could see pine-studded hillsides of compacted sand. It all reminded him of some place he had never seen, some place he would never know. Ever. The air was noticeably cooler and he shivered.

Fumarole looked at his watch. Moisture had condensed inside the crystal. He swirled the remainder of the liquor in the bottle. But did not drink it. "We're getting close to Da Lat."

"Is the train running close to schedule?"

"I wouldn't know about that. There never was a schedule after the French left. All I know is that it's a little over half a bottle from Phan Rang to the outskirts of Da Lat."

The ARVN aspirant had been sitting with his back against the open door. Suddenly he shouted something at the PF soldier beside him and pointed excitedly at something moving in the fog. The PF soldier cheeked his carbine, but did not fire. He had not changed magazines. The aspirant snatched the carbine from the PF and pulled a fresh magazine from the bandolier around the man's shoulders. He pressed the magazine release and the empty magazine slid out of its well, hit the floor of the car and spun away into space. The aspirant thrust home the fresh magazine, kneeling and working the charging handle to chamber a round. Then, still kneeling, he fired furiously into the fog. When the magazine was empty he peered intently into the damp grayness, stooping even lower until his face was almost level with the floor, as if he could see under the fog.

"What did you see?" Knox asked.

The aspirant spoke to them for the first time. "Maybe nothing, but if VC they plenty scared. I fire, scare them shit-less."

"They aren't the only ones," Knox said.

"Fuck an A," Fumarole said. "Only my houseboy will ever
know how scared I was."

The train finally got to Da Lat. Knox stood in the doorway
after the grade smoothed and the train picked up speed,
watching the pines flick past, the occasional villa, highland
rice fields and the waning sun still screened by the scud of
fog.

Fumarole had not touched the bottle again, but had eaten a
banana and given one each to the PFs. He had pointedly ignored the aspirant, and now the aspirant was ignoring him.
And then the train slowed, or at any rate changed the tempo
of its movement, as shacks of tarpaper and cardboard along
the right-of-way slid by with increasing slowness until they
were not sliding anymore and they were in Da Lat.

Fumarole pointed to a small group of people sitting and
standing by two late-model commerical jeeps. "Those are our
people." He slung his kit bag over one shoulder and hefted
the assault rifle. Knox followed, feeling very conspicious with
his large suitcase. They left the train without a backward
glance. The camera kept hitting Knox solidly in the ribs so he
took it from around his neck and carried it in one hand.

"This is Smith," Fumarole said. The smaller of the two non-
descript Americans standing by one jeep nodded. The other
introduced himself as Sweeney. They shook hands around.
Sweeney indicated a crew-cut Vietnamese in laundered tiger-
stripe camouflage fatigues with the three silver apricot blos-
soms of a full colonel on his collar.

"This is Colonel Hiep, the Province Chief."

The Province Chief did not offer to shake hands. He did
not look especially happy. "I am sorry to state that there
has been a very disturbing factor just reported to me." He

spoke slowly, with only a slight trace of an accent and with very good inflection, the result of Army Command and Staff School at Fort Leavenworth, probably, thought Knox. Sweeney looked embarrassed. Smith scuffed wet dirt with his shoe.

"There has been a report that a local elephant, in fact one belonging to the Da Lat Zoo, has been killed by vandals riding the train which just arrived."

"One of the soldiers on the train fired at something in the fog, but that was all the shooting done," said Fumarole.

"Don't forget the shooting just before the roadblock," Knox said.

"That wasn't close to Da Lat," Fumarole said.

Knox looked back toward the train. One of the PF soldiers had just kicked the Honda to life. He mounted the machine and the other soldier, holding both carbines, got on behind him. The third soldier and the aspirant were nowhere in sight.

"The driver of the elephant was taking him to a timber-haul job for which he had been hired," Colonel Hiep said. "He came to me when his elephant was slaughtered."

"We're fucked," Fumarole said. "No matter how you look at it, we're fucked."

Colonel Hiep continued as if he had never been interrupted. "I have decide to determine the circumstances of the killing. I am forming an Elephant Investigation Committee. Mr. Smith of the USAID and Mr. Sweeney of the Political Advisory Group informed me two United States peoples would be on the train." He glanced sideways at Knox. "It is fortunate one of you is a reporter. You can take pictures." Colonel Hiep looked at all of them in turn. "You are all part of my committee. My staff has already gone before us with the driver of the elephant to the scene of the murder." He stepped into his jeep. Fumarole and Knox got into the other jeep with Smith. The jeep with Colonel Hiep and Sweeney was already in motion.

"What in hell happened on the way up here?" Smith asked.

"Beats the bloody hell out of me," Fumarole said. "The frigging Viets were shooting off their guns every five minutes or so. They could have slaughtered a whole herd of elephants in that fog."

"Were they using American weapons?"

"What do you think?"

"They might have borrowed that AK forty-seven you're always carrying. If there's a dead elephant and if it was killed with American bullets it'll add up to our responsibility."

"Wouldn't have done that damn aspirant who did most of the shooting any good to use my gun. It's not loaded." Fumarole rapped the butt of the AK-47.

"You mean you've been carrying that damn thing all the way from Phan Rang and it's not loaded?" asked Knox.

"I don't have cartridge one for it. It's strictly for show."

Knox felt distinctly uneasy. "Then why do you carry it?"

"Because someone is always trying to buy it off me. You'd be surprised how many Tu Do Street commandos want one of these things. I get a good price for it, too."

"You sell it to more than one person?"

"Good God, no. I have a whole case of the damn things. Got them off a VC supply ship the Navy ran aground north of Nha Trang. Don't shoot them, though. Too much noise for me."

They were careening through the streets of Da Lat. Knox caught a glimpse of himself in the outside mirror. He felt for a comb but found none. The Vietnamese driver in the jeep ahead charged through crowds with a fine disregard for pedestrians. He was blowing the horn every time he twisted the steering wheel. The jeep slipped sideways in a patch of mud before the tires caught and flung it through.

"But that aspirant used a carbine. Hell, those bullets aren't powerful enough to kill an elephant," said Knox.

"They're solids. Don't expand. He shot a whole magazineful. If he did hit an elephant, chances are he killed it."

Fifteen minutes out of Da Lat by jeep on rutted, barely passable road, the lead vehicle pulled off into a thicket. The fog was still hanging in pockets here. Smith would have missed the turning had not a Vietnamese private in battle dress marked the place.

Colonel Hiep's jeep was parked a hundred meters off the road by another jeep in a stand of young pines. A short distance away Knox saw the embankment of the railroad. A small elephant lay on its side against a sapling bent at a sharp angle from its weight. Its visible eye was red rimmed, and it watched cautiously as the Elephant Investigation Committee dismounted from their jeeps. Otherwise the animal did not move. Colonel Hiep picked his way carefully through the damp sand. Unlike most high-ranking Vietnamese he wore carefully polished boots cut in the French pattern. He cautiously tapped the elephant on the foreleg with a length of bamboo. The elephant did not move. Then he kicked it hard between the toes. The elephant's trunk twitched feebly and Colonel Hiep quickly took a step backward.

"As you can plainly see the elephant is nearly dead. Plainly to all he was shot with American munition."

Knox walked over and stood peering down at the elephant. "I can't see any bullet wounds, Colonel Hiep, how can you be sure an American bullet hit this animal?"

Colonel Hiep arched his brows. Sweeney moved over by Knox. "A most good point," Colonel Hiep said. "Elephant is indeed laying on wounded side. Therefore we must turn the elephant on his other side."

"How in hell are we going to turn this thing over?" asked Sweeney.

Colonel Hiep motioned to a small, thin Viet with a wisp of gray beard and cataract-milky eyes, whom Knox guessed was the mahout. They stood in animated conversation for several moments, then Colonel Hiep turned to them: "The driver will order the elephant to roll over."

The mahout called to the elephant in sharp, gutteral tones. The elephant moved its trunk but that was all. The mahout gave the order again. He prodded it behind the ear with the bamboo he took from Colonel Hiep. The elephant did not twitch its trunk this time. The mahout turned to Colonel Hiep and shrugged.

"There is a Signal Corps detachment at Da Lat," Smith said. "They have a five-ton wrecker. We could get that, and some cable."

"I say we give it up as a lost cause," Sweeney said. "The elephant is obviously" — he stopped and groped for a word — "displaying a dying syndrome."

"At the present the elephant's condition seems to counter-indicate a continuance of life-support functions," Fumarole said. His hand was resting on his kit bag, above the bulge which was the bottle of Johnny Walker.

"It's an obvious waste of time to stand around here any longer," Sweeney said. "Why don't we go ahead and dis-patch the elephant?"

Knox looked toward the embankment and saw that some Meo tribesmen had gathered at the edge of the fog. He had not heard them come up.

"That is not a matter for the Investigation Committee," Colonel Hiep said. "That will be the recommendation of the Elephant Execution Committee. Soon I will decide to name the committee."

"Well, why not put it out of its misery now and let it go at that?" Knox asked.

Sweeney was annoyed. Knox did not know if it was because of him or the Meo tribesmen. "You'll have to excuse this man, Colonel Hiep, he's just arrived in your country. He does not yet know how we do things here."

"That is perfectly all right, I presume you. But first I must have the satisfaction of the committee the elephant is dying."

Sweeney answered for all of them. "Yes, Colonel, the committee is satisfied the elephant is dying."

"And is the committee satisfied that the weapon which caused the wound was an American weapon?"

Knox started to say something, but Sweeney stepped on his foot.

"It is settle then. Obviously since an American weapon was used the American government must accept consequences for the unfortunate incident. I must now charge your government with a claim." Col Hiep was secure in the supremacy of his own logic. "Now all that remain is to name an execution committee. I shall do that tomorrow." Colonel Hiep turned and walked to his jeep.

"Aren't you going to kill the elephant now?" asked Knox.

"Not indeed. There are papers. Many papers. By the zoo, at the district, at the province, not to say the Head of the Animal Husbandry Service must be notified. We must coordinate many matters. The elephant was beloved by many people in Da Lat. They come to see him long time. Many peoples are involved."

"But in the meantime the elephant is just laying here. How would you like to be in his place?"

Sweeney was really pressing hard on Knox's foot.

"But obviously I am not the elephant and the elephant is not me. If he was to have been killed then he should have been killed when the peoples on the train shoot him." Again he was smug in the sheer brilliance of his logic. He looked at Sweeney for confirmation. "I cannot be responsible for what someone else failed to do."

Sweeney got into the back of Colonel Hiep's jeep and they drove off. The circle of Meos parted quietly to let them through. Then closed again. The remaining Vietnamese soldiers and the mahout got into their jeep and followed. Leaving only Knox, Fumarole and Smith.

Fumarole walked over to one of the tribesmen and motioned toward the long triangular French bayonet meticulously wired to a shaft of ironwood for a spear. The tribesman reluctantly gave it to him. Fumarole placed the point of the spear behind the juncture of the foreleg with the barrel and leaned his weight against the shaft. The bayonet vanished into the wrinkled gray skin, hesitated for a moment when the juncture of wood and wire met resistance, then slid in with increasing difficulty. The elephant squealed like a pig and its legs thrashed convulsively. A thin trickle of blood came from the trunk, then it was silent. Its bowels loosened and some runny droppings coursed down its flank. The Meo tribesmen clapped their hands. One of them rushed in and lopped off the trunk with several blows of a machete. He threw it over his shoulder and ran off. The rest of the Meos closed in and began chopping frantically at the elephant. Knox tasted bile in the back of his throat.

Fumarole left the spear in the elephant. Smith shook his head. "Now you've really screwed up the whole business. Sweeney will have your ass for this."

"Let him. He won't bust no cherry."

"Why did that old man run away with the trunk first thing?" Knox asked.

Fumarole kicked some wet sand from his shoes before getting into the jeep. "Something to do with potency. Just like tiger dick and rhino horn. These people believe that elephant trunk puts lead in their pencil. They believe it so it must be true for them. All you have to do is believe in something enough and it's true."

"Fine. I don't believe I'm here."

"Right you are. We're in the fucking Moulin Rouge getting our gut wrenches torqued out of shape."

Some of the elephant's ribs were showing dull white through the froth of bloody meat. Knox got into the back of the jeep and Smith switched on the ignition. A Meo trotted up to the jeep. He had succeeded in severing one of the elephant's forefeet and he staggered under its weight. "Hey, GI, you take." He hefted the meat into the back seat. The muddy foot with its big nails fell heavily on the seat and splattered them all with blood. Knox tried to throw it out.

"Tahe! Tahe! All Mericans want foots." The Meo grinned delightedly, disclosing great gaps between his yellowed, ferretlike teeth. Fumarole waved and Smith drove away. Knox waited until they were safely on the road toward Da Lat before pitching the foot into some tall saw grass.

"Why didn't Colonel Hiep appoint a Meat Distribution Committee?"

"That was probably next on his list," Smith said.

"Well, we saved him the trouble." Fumarole rummaged in his kit bag. "Damn, one of these fucking Montagnards pinched my bottle."

III

Sweeney was plainly angry. "You may have ruined two years of hard work. My work. A liaison with Hiep I worked my balls off to build. And you screw up the whole job because of one rotten elephant."

"Its death wasn't our fault. We still don't know if it was shot or not. No one even saw a bullet hole. Why do we have to pay for it, much less say we are responsible?" Fumarole had deserted Knox in favor of something to eat and a hot bath, both at Smith's quarters in the USAID compound. On top of that, Colonel Hiep's driver was bargaining for Fumarole's AK-47; he had the man up to twenty thousand piastres already. So Knox had to face Sweeney alone.

"You school types are all alike. No concept of political realities. Come busting out here thinking you know all there is to know. When I've spent two fucking years of my goddamn life in this hole trying to make something out of our involvement. I'm just about to get the Phoenix program off the ground, and just when the Province Chief begins trusting me you bust it up with your Boy Scout act." Sweeney was breathing heavily. He had very little hair and his entire head was flushed. He gestured futilely and sat down in the rickety folding chair behind his desk.

"Look at you. You look like you were caught in a mudslide then took a bath in an abattoir."

"You wanted to see me right away. I didn't have time to clean up." Knox was trying to answer mildly. "A soft answer turneth away wrath." He repeated the phrase to himself. It was all he could recall from countless Sunday mornings in Sunday School. He never had liked Sunday School.

Only the phrase did not work. "That's no damn excuse. You represent the Agency twenty-four hours a day. Same as me."

Knox held up his camera. It had elephant blood smeared on the lens cover. "I'm supposed to be a reporter on this trip. What does it matter what people think of me if they also think I'm a reporter?"

"You think Hiep didn't have you pegged as CAS right from the minute you got off the train? You're dead wrong. You're supposed to be a goddamn reporter and you didn't take a single goddamn picture out there.

"You and that goddamn Fumarole. He carries an empty rifle and you carry an empty camera. Who in shit knew you had no film in the goddamn thing? Just snap away, click a few to fake it for the Viets." Sweeney paused for breath. Knox's face was tingling with something that was not quite embarrassment, not quite frustration.

Sweeney sighed heavily and waved an arm in vague dismissal. "Go on. Get out of here. Get cleaned up. Talking to you is like pissing on a duck. We're having an operational briefing tonight. Get some sleep, then be there. I know you're up here to check on me, so I want you to be in on all the plans. Fumarole knows where it'll be. And stay out of Hiep's way."

Knox went out. Deliberately walking slowly so more mud drying and falling off his shoes would flake onto the floor of Sweeney's office. He was trying to be perverse, even insolent. It did not work. Very little mud fell off. The floor was dirty anyway.

He found Fumarole in the USAID compound shooting craps with Colonel Hiep's driver. The Vietnamese had the AK-47 leaning against the wall behind him. "Where do I go for a bath and someplace to sleep?"

Fumarole jerked his head in the direction of a Vietnamese

in dirty blue jeans who was reading a comic book. Fumarole did not take his eyes from the dice. "He'll take you to the visiting reporters' billet. USAID's got a nice hotel for members of the journalistic profession. Working stiffs like me got to flop down where they can." He paused to scoop up some money — well, piastres then. Knox had not yet come to think of piastres as money. "I'll come by and get you for the briefing tonight."

"Okay." And almost as an afterthought. "Who's winning?"

"I almost got my AK forty-seven back."

"How much did you get for it?"

"Twenty five thou."

"I didn't think a driver made that much."

"They have other income." Fumarole did not elaborate.

Knox got his suitcase and told the barefooted Vietnamese where he wanted to go and followed him out of the compound, across the street, around the corner and down two more streets and into the courtyard of a pink, two story villa. The Vietnamese took him to the second floor, to a spacious room with a small iron-frame hospital bed and a mosquito bar. There had been a reception desk on the first floor, but no clerk, and the Vietnamese seemed to know where to go anyway. The only other furniture was a wardrobe and a single wicker chair. A bathroom with French plumbing, including a bidet, was visible through a door to the left. A cool breeze slipped into the room without stirring the curtains. Two flies followed some invisible track sensed only by them across the floor in procession. The Vietnamese was waiting for a tip, but Knox had carried his own suitcase all the way from the USAID compound so he said, "Thank you very much," and ignored the man. After a while the Viet gave up and went away.

Knox took a shower in lukewarm water. And then went

to sleep on the hospital bed as soon as he had toweled dry.
He was awakened by screams and loud voices down the
hallway. He opened his eyes with effort and got to his feet.
His dirty clothes were still where he had dropped them and
he almost tripped. The shrieks were louder now and he
could hear a male voice speaking in English. He found the
wet towel and wrapped it around his waist, then peered
cautiously into the hallway. A Vietnamese girl in black *nha
que* pantaloons was struggling with a bearded American.

The girl heard the door open and looked around at Knox.
"Help me," she said. "He fuck me with rubber." Then the
girl said something in Vietnamese and the American cuffed
her across the mouth, then the cheek. Her flesh showed
crimson from the blows; but she stopped screaming. He led
her away by the arms, holding her tightly, hustling her
away in quick, rapid steps. Knox could not tell if she looked
back. The American pushed her down the staircase and
Knox heard nothing further. He was still very tired. He
closed the door and went back to sleep with the towel still
wrapped around him.

Fumarole woke him in the short twilight which preceded
the descent of darkness in the tropics. It was still hot and
Fumarole smelled very much of liquor.

Knox got out of bed and stretched. He wanted more
sleep badly. But he began pulling clothes from his suitcase.
They went out to the jeep parked by the sandbagged kiosk
where the Nung guard stood with his shotgun resting over
the top of the sandbags. He saluted them awkwardly and
Fumarole returned the salute. Just as awkwardly. They got
into the jeep and Fumarole unlocked the wheel. He
dropped the chain on the floorboard and snapped the lock
through a spoke. They drove down the darkened streets
and one woman in peasant trousers and straw hat tied

under her chin turned to look at them. Without hostility. Without passion. Without anything but the acknowledgment in her dull inscrutability of their passing.

Sweeney was standing beside a large easel with a covered map resting on it when they entered the large sandbagged tent inside the USAID compound. There were no chairs in the tent so they joined the small semicircle of Americans in civilian clothes and Army fatigues standing before the easel, faces as intent and pale as the dead bellies of fish. Sweeney did not look at Knox.

Colonel Hiep strolled into the tent. He had four ARVN officers with him, some other Vietnamese and a Cambodian with a Meo tribal bracelet of crude brass on his wrist. His party filled the tent. Sweeney frowned and spoke to Hiep in a low voice, but everybody in the tent heard him anyway. "Damn it, Colonel Hiep, we've got too many people here."

"But Mister Sweeney need I must remind you we of necessity have to bring the peoples from Interrogations, the Police Special Branch, the psywar peoples and the Census-Grievance Committee. And how can this work without the actual eyes of the PRU who brought in the defectors?" Hiep pointed to two Vietnamese of below-average height who were huddled together. They appeared to be under no restraint, but the Cambodian was watching them closely.

Sweeney swallowed his irritation. He flipped back the blank cover of the map and rapped his pointer across the paper for attention. "Three days ago one of the PRUs operating between here and Cambodia brought in two low-level defectors from a Cong village fifty-sixty ks from here. Duc Buon, to be exact." Sweeney described a vague area on the map with equally vague motions of his pointer. "These people were interviewed by Colonel Hiep's Police Special Branch. We have identified some of the Viet Cong infrastructure in this village as a result of these interviews. We are mounting a Phoenix Operation against this village to detain the VC cadre identified."

Throughout the briefing Knox heard people moving past the tent. He turned his head once and saw an American walk by, then a Vietnamese *nha que*.

Sweeney continued. "Because of the size of the hamlet and its distance from here we have called for assistance from II Corps. They have furnished two companies of troops from Fire Support Base Hilda." Sweeney tapped a spot on the map, but not really long enough for anyone to see where he pointed. "They'll rendezvous with us here in assault helicopters and we'll proceed to the LZ. The Army will secure the LZ and cordon off the village. Police Special Branch and PRUs will take care of actual operations in the village. We'll have the two defectors along to point out the cadre. Anybody identified will be detained."

Sweeney looked around the tent expectantly. Daring them to ask questions. An Army major did. "Would you give me the coordinates for tomorrow's rendezvous?"

Sweeney looked at the map and called off some figures. The major copied them onto the back of his hand with grease pencil. "When do you want us there?"

"I want you there at o-seven hundred hours sharp so we can be on the ground at Duc Buon by o-seven-fifteen."

"We'll try to make it, but the flying from Base Hilda is rough. Lotta fog that time of the morning. And we'll have to fly low."

"Are you saying you can't make it on time?"

The Army major squirmed uncomfortably. "I'm saying we'll try to make it. If we can't you'll just have to orbit until we get there."

"Well for God's sake try to be on time, Major. This is a

big operation." Sweeney turned to Colonel Hiep. "Have you anything to add, Colonel?"

Hiep spoke to the Vietnamese. His voice shrill as most Vietnamese's are when they speak rapidly. Arrogant with the assurance that he possessed the most important qualification for position, seeming loyalty to the party in power. The Cambodian got a running translation in French from one of the staff officers. Knox shifted restlessly. The Army major shifted position also and picked his nose. Colonel Hiep finished speaking and tapped the map board several times for emphasis. For good measure he also called off a few grid coordinates of his own.

Sweeney started talking again. First to the Army major. "Be at the rendezvous coordinates at o-seven hundred or I'll have to send Westmoreland a message about your inability to conform to our planning. It's important we catch this village by surprise." The major flushed angrily. Then to the rest of his audience: "Anybody got any questions?" No one said anything. "All right then, the Army provides perimeter security. Special Police and PRUs do the actual house-to-house searches. The rest of us will be along for observation only." He looked significantly at Knox. "That's all, gentlemen. Takeoff time for us is o-six-forty. Everyone in place by o-six-twenty for marshaling."

The meeting ended. Colonel Hiep stood talking to one of his staff officers. He broke off and looked at Fumarole. "I have been given to understand that the elephant belonging to the zoo died soon after my visit this afternoon. And the meat was distributed without the planning of a Meat Distribution Committee. I was also given to understand that the meat went to the Moi."

"Is that so, Colonel Hiep? I'm sorry to hear that. The elephant looked like he would survive when we left."

"Perhaps. But he was stuck with a Moi spear."

"Then obviously the Moi must have killed him. The Moi were there. They had spears. Obviously the Moi killed the elephant."

"Yes, I am sure that was the case." Hiep turned to Knox. "And are you to accompany us on the Phung Hoang tomorrow?"

"Yessir. I'm going to cover it for my paper."

"What paper is that?"

"Well actually, Colonel Hiep, I'm what you might call a stringer. I send material to several Stateside papers. You have never heard of them."

"Is one of them in Kansas?"

"One of them is in Kansas."

"Good. Send a picture of me to that one. I was at the US Army Staff School at Fort Leavenworth. They still remember me there." Then quickly to Fumarole: "You do not like elephant meat, Mr. Fumarole?"

"I do not know, Colonel. I have never tried it."

"That is too bad. The trunk is especially good. Many peoples past middle age, superstitious peoples, will do anything to get it. They consider it an aid to potency."

"I have children of my own, Colonel; I don't consider myself impotent."

Hiep smiled at them. "Au voir, gentlemens." He beckoned to his staff and they fell in step behind him as he left the tent.

Smith came over and joined them. "Anyone care for something to eat? There's a field ration mess on the other side of the compound."

"I could use something solid," Fumarole said. "My mouth feels like a whole Vietnamese Army walked through it."

They drove in Smith's jeep over to the Army Field Ration Mess where they paid, signed the chit sheet and got some greasy spam and cheese sandwiches and bitter coffee in thick white enamel mugs.

"How did Hiep find out about that damn elephant?"

"Don't think he's not a smart little sonabitch. You don't stay in the power group for long unless you have a few smarts. He ain't no rookie."

"You'll need some film for that camera," Smith said. "Sweeney told me you didn't have any. It would help back at the Station if you have some pictures to show. You'd better get something to wear besides that white shirt. You'll stand out like a whore in Sunday School."

Knox looked down at his clothes. "Okay. Get me some clothes so I'll look like a real Boy Scout. Let me know how much I owe you."

"No charge. I'm going to steal them from the Army."

IV

They jumped off at 0640 the next morning. Knox was still sleepy. The PRUs were sitting on the edge of the runway at the military airstrip. About where the Caribou cargo planes would touch down. They would move to the middle of the runway whenever a plane turned on final for landing and sit there in the early morning light, barely visible in their green battle dress, ducking their heads only when the landing gear was about to strike them. The last man to duck his head was the winner of the game. Sometimes the cargo pilots would not play the game, though, and would land further down the strip. Then all the PRUs would laugh as if it were the greatest game in the world.

Knox was dressed in ill-fitting jungle fatigues. He had film canisters in the slash pockets of his blouse. He was wearing a steel helmet with the words CORRESPONDENT and

BAO CHI crudely lettered in felt marker across the slitted front of the camouflage cover. There was something wrong with one of the helicopters sitting off by themselves on their own rectangular pads of pierced steel planking. Sweeney was worried they would not make the takeoff on time. He stood talking to Colonel Hiep, but from time to time he glanced over at the team of mechanics, already shirtless despite the morning chill of the highlands, working on the turbine of the Huey. Fumarole was half-dozing against the bulk of his kit bag on a dry patch of pierced steel. The dew had wet all the grass, and the boots and trouser legs of the men were already dark with it where they had walked through the grass. Fumarole had won back the AK-47 from Hiep's driver and traded it to an Army Spec-4 for an M-16 and fifty dollars. He had the M-16 propped casually across his chest. A bandolier of magazines was strapped around his waist and even though Knox had not seen it yet he knew Fumarole had a bottle of whiskey somewhere in the kit bag.

The mechanics finally pronounced the Huey fit and they scrambled into the helicopters, eight men to a copter, ten Vietnamese because they were smaller. Knox sat up front just behind the two warrant officers flying the Huey. The left-door gunner snapped the webbing across the door and swiveled his M-60 machine gun experimentally. Wherever Knox went he seemed to be always behind a machine gun in a doorway. They lifted off smoothly in the deafening clatter of the chopper blades.

They flew for five minutes in a fairly straight line and then the five helicopters formed into a loose arrowhead with one copter leading and the others spread out two on either side like some grotesque V of pregnant metallic geese. One of the warrant officers unsnapped his seat belt and crawled back into the troop compartment. He fished out a thermos and poured coffee into a plastic cup, blowing on the coffee to cool it and balancing himself against the motion of the Huey as nonchalantly as if he were on a picnic. The left-door gunner had his finger outside the trigger guard of the M-60 and every now and again he traversed the barrel to train the muzzle on something only he could see. He was very nervous. Knox said so to the warrant officer.

"He should be. He's going home soon. No more of this shit for him."

"He looks young to be in the Army," Knox said. The warrant officer did not look much older.

"He's nineteen," the warrant officer said. "I'm twenty-four."

One of the PRUs said something to a Nung. The door gunner looked fearfully at the PRU. His finger moved from the guard to the trigger.

"I'm a reporter," Knox said. "You want me to get you in a picture?"

The warrant officer grimaced and the ends of his mustache bunched around the corners of his mouth. "Naw. I've been in plenty. And besides, this is the slopes' show. Every time we have CBS or NBC along for an operation the company commander asks who hasn't been on TV. It gets old after a while. No offense, buddy, but we got too many reporters out here. Sometimes they put guys up to doing things they wouldn't do, not in a million years otherwise." He looked uncomfortable as he spoke and pulled off his helmet to massage the back of his neck.

"Such things as what?" Knox said.

"Well, sometimes you get real upset, know what I mean? I mean, not being able to tell one slope from another. That gives you a real bad feeling. You tend to get tight when your buddy's hit by ambush the villagers in the place you just passed could have told you about, but didn't tell you about. Know what I mean? You get real tight. And then sometimes there's so much hollering and screaming and people getting all worked up and everybody's raising a whole bunch of hell and you look down at your best buddy who's just been blown in half by a RPG and you just kinda go blank. Know what I mean? And somebody's putting a knife in your hand and there's a Cong prisoner somebody picked up and next thing you know you're on that bastard and trying to cut off an ear or a nut or else kill him because his kind just killed your best buddy, and you got enough hate in you for the whole fucking world. Know what I mean? And all the time, some reporter who put the knife in your hand all the time is standing out of the way and taking pictures of all this for his papers." The warrant officer lapsed into silence and chewed the ends of his mustache like an old man.

Knox was silent too and looked out at the trees and neat little fields passing below. The sun was up good now and most of the early morning fog was burning away.

The warrant officer gestured toward the door. "There are the other choppers." He checked his watch. "More or less on time, too."

Fumarole pushed up his hat and squinted into the early morning sun. He also checked his watch. "Hot damn, that must be a first. He slipped his hand into the kit bag and brought out a bottle of Pinch. "Such punctuality calls for a drink." He unscrewed the cap and took a long pull. His Adam's apple bobbed three times before he lowered the bottle and offered it to the WO. The WO drank the coffee dregs in his cup and splashed in a slug of the liquor. He glanced over his shoulder. The copilot was intent on the gauges and pedals. He swallowed the whiskey and smacked his lips. "Beats that homebrew we have to make from rice." He still squatted on his haunches, jiggling the cup.

"How much farther?"

"Another ten minutes."

And so they twittered on in the abrasiveness of their relationships. The door gunner nervous and wary of the Vietnamese and the Vietnamese apprehensive in their knowledge of possible violent contact with some men much like themselves who might very shortly be attempting to take their lives. Everyone now silent in his own cloistered cell of introspection, undergoing his own catharsis before battle, and doubting the dependability of the men around him. With the fierce tattoo of drum rolls toward nowhere sounding in their brains.

Knox thought back to the briefing of the night before, that ritualistic drama of noncommunication redolent with its own knowing jargon. Staged like a minuscule war of its own, replete with detailed planning, pursued with equal energy as actual combat, and perhaps even tabulated in terms of people briefed to death. The optimism which alternated with bewilderment, the euphoria which gave way to frustration. He knew, or rather felt innately, that the operation would be nothing more than a repeat of the briefing. And it could all be reckoned as nothing more than an exercise in futility. Except that perhaps there would be some fighting, and some people might be killed.

Knox checked his camera and felt in his blouse pockets for the extra cans of film. He also felt the great half-moons of perspiration beneath his armpits and the prickle of sweat between his shoulders. His stomach and diaphragm were tensed and he was breathing shallowly, but rapidly. His lungs felt as if they were just below his throat.

Fumarole pointed out the door just as the copilot tapped the WO on the shoulder and the WO clambered back into his seat. "There's the village. Hang tight. We're going in fast to avoid ground fire."

They came in low over the tops of some banana trees and

hovered just above grass level in a field a quarter of a mile from the nearest house. "Let's go, sport, and you'd better learn to undo that belt before we get this close again." Knox leaped out and promptly bogged down in ankle-deep mud. The PRUs were ahead of him, running heavily across the field toward the first huts. He got to his feet but was staggered again by the downblast from the rotors. Other copters were disgorging their troops. An American soldier ran by him and a moment later fired his M-16 on full automatic. The sound was like that of a large metallic kitten purring. Knox remembered to keep his head down and ran like a crab across the grass and sucking mud. Holding his camera out from him like a weapon.

He heard more firing and looked around, but the shooting was all behind him as the Army troops secured the perimeter. And he could not look for the shooting and watch where he was going at the same time. He wanted to prostrate himself full length in the mud, to get as low as possible, but everyone else was still on his feet so Knox kept running, too. His lungs ached as a diver's must when coming up too quickly from too deep a dive.

Helicopters were still settling down all over the field. The Army troops had deployed to the line of trees edging the field. He supposed the LZ was secure now. At least most of the shooting had stopped. Knox wished the Army troops were up front ahead of him and not the PRUs. Because his head was down, he charged full tilt into a hut and dislodged a bamboo pole supporting the porch.

Two PRUs were already in the house and they whirled about with carbines thrust forward. Then they returned to peering intently out the crude window toward the rest of the hamlet. There was no more firing. After a few minutes Knox saw some PRUs walking toward the hamlet along a well-defined path. Walking. Not running. They were moving warily with rifles waist high. He waited until they were almost into the village outskirts. There was still no firing, so Knox followed them.

Fumarole saw him and waved. Knox returned the wave and even snapped a few pictures. He saw an old woman squatting stoically in front of her farmhouse. Her drawn, seamed face was almost framed by her thin knees and the ground around her was speckled with betel-nut stains. A Special Police was boiling duck eggs on her mud stove. Two more PRUs were amusing themselves by knocking holes in *nuoc mam* pots with their rifle butts. Knox walked on.

He found Colonel Hiep with Sweeney and a small knot of other functionaries. Hiep was shaking his head sadly and saying, "VC *di di*," to one of his staff officers. Fumarole came up and handed Knox some roughly printed leaflets he had found snagged on a bush.

"Government propaganda," Fumarole said. "Probably dropped by psywar planes late yesterday. Couldn't have chosen a better time if they'd tried."

Some PRUs were walking by a row of mud bunkers. They were pinning leaflets they carried in plastic bags slung from their canteen belts onto the walls of the houses and tree trunks. Knox took a picture of the mud bunkers.

"From the looks of those bunkers this really must be a Cong redoubt," said Knox. The bunkers were low, but deep, and blended in well with the rest of the ground like shadows. Some of the more cautious Special Police were leapfrogging from bunker to bunker.

"Doesn't mean a damn thing," Fumarole said. "This is a free strike zone. Any plane with unexpended ordnance can dump it on this village. You'd have a bunker, too, if you lived here."

They reached the center of the village and found that

Colonel Hiep had set up his command post in the square. At one time the market had been covered and shops and market stalls had surrounded it. But now it was burned out. Hiep pointed to a triangular block of concrete ringed with skeins of concertina wire. The block was surmounted by a piece of helicopter rotor blade. The monument was some twelve feet high and was situated in the exact geometrical center of the square.

"VC monument. You take pictures please." Knox obediently snapped several pictures. He even moved around and took some from different angles.

"What does this damn thing commemorate?"

"The shooting down of a helicopter," Fumarole said. "Some Charlie gunner got a bicycle and a month's pass in the deal. His local unit most likely threw up this piece of junk to celebrate the achievement."

Two Special Police were attaching demolition strips of gel-ignite to the base and halfway up the sides of the monument. Another was running thin electrical wires back to a small hand-held detonator. The two Special Police finished strapping the charges in place and scurried away. They had been pretty efficient. And the wires were not attached to the detonator until they were clear. Pretty good. For Vietnamese. The other Special Police handed the detonator to Colonel Hiep. A staff officer blew a whistle and everybody took cover. Colonel Hiep spun the handle of the detonator and the monument disintegrated under the implosion of the charges. A thick pall of acrid smoke and dust hung in the still air. Some of it settled on Knox and stuck to his skin and clothes in a fine paste.

A priest in white vestments came out of the church across the square. Hiep walked over with pistol drawn. The priest stood waiting calmly with hands folded in front of him. Knox could see that the church was freshly painted. The cross which surmounted the small cupola had been struck by a piece of shrapnel from the demolition of the VC monument and was leaning askew.

Hiep was talking to the priest in rapid Vietnamese. The priest heard him out and answered calmly. Knox edged around the two men and glanced inside the church. An irregular double row of bullet holes in the sheet-tin roof marked an earlier visit by a helicopter gunship or an A-1E. The shrapnel had also knocked out several windowpanes. But it was still very much a church. Orderly and clean. Freshly swept and the few missals arranged in neat, even piles on a bench in the rear.

Outside in the square the priest was being hustled away. A PRU was placing a black hood over the man's head. The priest's hands were already tied and someone had tagged him with a neatly printed detainee card run through a fold of his cassock with thin copper wire with the ends twisted. His white vestments had been shucked off and thrown in a rumpled heap in the shadow of the church. Several other detainees were already squatting in a small circle under a chinaberry tree. Some of them had hoods. Some did not. A guard made the priest sit down in the group.

Knox took a picture of that, too. They looked for all the world like a pathetic klavern of Ku Klux Klansmen. But he did not feel like laughing.

The high-pitched twitter of rotors and a shadow fleeing briefly across the square marked the arrival of a helicopter. It set down like a huge dragonfly in the middle of the square where the monument acclaiming the destruction of another of its kind had stood until recently. The blades threw up a cloud of dust and everybody turned their backs to the blast. Knox covered his nose with the collar of his fatigue blouse. But it did no good. He still got a lot of grit in his nose and mouth. The major who had been at the briefing the night before got out of the helicopter. He seemed pleased with himself. He joined Colonel Hiep and Sweeney and spread open a map with plastic overlay marked by red grease pencil.

"We zapped five Charlies trying to get through the cordon."

"We haven't done much here," Sweeney said. "They must have got word we were coming. All the troops are gone. There's been no return fire. Only men left in the hamlet are old men and the priest."

The major frowned. "Sounds like something got screwed up somewhere. Maybe that briefing of yours last night. There was a whole shitpot full of people moving around outside."

Sweeney glared at him. They conferred another minute or two and then the major departed. Again in dust and last year's dried leaves.

Some of the PRUs were eating food they had taken from houses. One had disposed of all his psywar leaflets and was using the heavy plastic bag to hold vegetables and a live chicken. It made an awkward bundle. Particularly since the chicken was thrashing and kicking spasmodically. The operation was taking on a festive air.

A Special Police came up from the direction of the river to report he had found the marks of a lot of sampans along the bank. Sweeney received the news dourly. "That explains why no draft-age men are around. The able bodies were warned and took off."

Fumarole was eating a crab apple. He passed one to Knox and Knox took a bite, then spat it out. "They just had to have their big briefing last night," Fumarole said. "Hell, if I had known Sweeney was going to let Hiep pretend to run this show I wouldn't have come. And fuck what the Station said. Put that in your report to Balfour."

Knox said nothing.

Sweeney and Smith were questioning a woman just added to the group of prisoners. The Special Police interpreter was not very expert. The woman looked at them sullenly.

"How much do the VC collect from you in taxes?"

"No know no VC," she said in broken English.

"Where did you learn your English?"

"In Da Nang. I work there many year."

"How much does the whole village pay, and don't lie to me."

"No know VC. Me Buddhist. Buddhist no know VC."

"How many times do the VC song teams come here?"

"No many."

"What do they say?"

"They say Americans get tired soon. Go home."

Sweeney shrugged and turned away. Knox was very thirsty. He had been looking for water for some time now but had seen none. Other than the canteens carried by the Vietnamese. He told Fumarole and Fumarole located a large pottery crock in one of the houses. Knox had to splash out the film of dust and mosquito larvae on top and drink from cupped hands. The water was lukewarm and tasted of things he did not like to think about.

Four Special Police were interrogating a man in the back of the house. One of them touched the man's feet from time to time with the bud of a lighted cigarette. They were all firing questions at the man without giving him time to answer. The man also had a thin woven cord of nylon holding his mouth open. One of the Special Police grabbed the man's hair and smashed his face against a table. Blood dripped from a split lip. An eye puffed almost shut.

Knox walked out of the house feeling as thirsty as he had before Fumarole showed him the crock. All the villagers the PRUs and Special Police had been able to locate were huddled in the square. A psywar lieutenant was standing on a basket and lecturing the old men and despondent women about the benevolence of the government in Saigon. Other Special Police were tacking up big posters of Ky and Thieu. Sweeney was standing with the two informers. They had hoods of their own made from rough burlap with slits cut for eyeholes. They pointed to people in the crowd and they were tied and led away to the growing band of detainees. The last man taken was so old he could not walk fast. His guard raised the man's bound arms behind him until the old man's torso was parallel to the ground. When that did not hurry the old man along and he stumbled the guard dragged him the rest of the way by his bound arms. He dumped the old man into the group of prisoners. The old man somehow managed to get his feet under him and squatted. His shaven head bobbed slightly from side to side with the effort of breathing. His eyes were closed.

"That's taking it pretty rough on the old man," Knox said.

"You never know," Smith said. "He could be the head Cong for the area."

Knox heard a shot from the house where he had found the water pot. He went back inside the house and saw the body of the Vietnamese who had been interrogated by the Special Police. The man's body twitched and a Special Police shot him again with the muzzle of the carbine pressed against the man's ear. The twitching stopped. The Special Police filed out past Knox and the last man struck a match to a pile of thatch in the corner by the water crock. The house burned readily.

Back in the square, the Census-Grievance people were returning identification cards to the people who had had them. The knot of prisoners had grown considerably. A swirl of hot wind blew out from the burning house and

Knox smelled the faint cinnamon odor of burned flesh. The priest was talking quietly to the old man through his hood. The old man's head was still bobbing steadily with a peculiar rhythm all its own.

"May as well get the hell out of here and see if Interrogations can get more from these people than we can," Sweeney said. Then to Smith: "What's the score?"

"Five KIAs shot running away, the major reported. Then one prisoner killed while trying to escape. That makes six in all. No friendly casualties."

Sweeney nodded. "Maybe we salvaged something after all."

"What do you think of Operation Phoenix?" Fumarole said.

"Like trying to root the Democrats out of Chicago," Knox said.

Fumarole did not comment, but stopped long enough to take a quick pull from his bottle. They got back into the helicopters which had returned to meet them. Knox was separated from Fumarole and got into the chopper with the priest and the old man and two Special Police interrogators. The chopper lifted off and soon they were high above the trees and Duc Buon and the risk of ground fire and heading toward Da Lat. The two interrogators went to work on the priest first, kneeling in the troop compartment and hammering at the priest with their fists while the door gunners looked the other way.

The priest took it all with bowed head. That enraged the Special Police. The old man was nodding still but his eyes were wide open. Knox gathered the torture was designed to get the old man to talk rather than the priest. The priest was not saying anything, except perhaps praying. The two Special Police had worked themselves into a frenzy. They were striking the priest with gun butts now, in the groin, and spitting on him. Shouting in their shrill language all the while. One of the door gunners pulled his helmet down closer over his ears. Suddenly one of the Special Police seized the priest by the legs and began dragging him toward the door. The other Special Police grabbed the priest's arms and in one mad rush tumbled him out the open door. Raising him over the safety webbing and causing the helicopter to wobble unsteadily in flight for a moment before the pilot corrected for it.

It all happened before Knox could swallow the sour spittle which had grown in his mouth. The old man began to babble rapidly in a voice which trailed off to a quaver. Knox settled back into himself and his eyes marched to the horizon and on into the sky lying prone and vanquished in the embrace of brooding desolation and enigmatic death. He thought about the priest just briefly and supposed he had met a better fate than he would have received at the National Interrogations Center, where prisoners were killed without pomp after the medical instruments and fishnets had done their work and buried in quicklime without circumstance. Make that seven VC KIA. Still no friendly casualties.

V

Knox returned to Saigon the next day. This time via an Air America U-10 Helicourier from Lien Khang Airport at Da Lat to the Air America terminal at Tan son Nhut, just across the road from the new MACV Headquarters which was being built, and which the reporters had already begun calling Pentagon East.

The flight was turbulent, and Knox was airsick part of the time. The little plane was vectored around an air strike west of Cam Ranh Bay, then a storm front caught them and the Air America pilot did a one-eighty and flew back to Cam Ranh to wait out the storm. Knox went inside the operations building and tried to call Saigon. He got as far as Saigon Port on a patch before the circuits became saturated, and he gave up in disgust. He sat in the ops building and drank the corrosive coffee found in all ops buildings and watched the helicopters landing in the rain and gusts of wind on the pad by the hospital; the raincoated attendants carrying in the litters, bending low to stay under the helicopter blades, then scuttling away like spiders with the litters suspended hammocklike between them, and now and again someone walking bent over alongside a litter, struggling to hold a plasma bottle in the wind.

It was still early evening when he got to Saigon, and he could not get through to the Embassy exchange. No one from CAS was expecting him so he caught a ride into Saigon on one of the illegal three-wheeled Lambretta minibuses because it had begun to rain lightly and no taxis passed.

The three-wheeled Lambretta jolted over the unpaved stretch of road just after they passed the Canh Sat checkpoint, and the bus was going so slowly that another American, a soldier with master sergeant's chevrons on his fatigues, climbed into the bus. He squeezed between two Vietnamese women in *nha que* hats and took off his fatigue cap. He grinned at Knox. "Don't want the MPs seeing me in one of these things."

They rode on in silence. Knox tried to breathe shallowly, as little as possible, but the acrid bite of the exhaust fumes welled up around him every time the Lambretta slowed. The green and white Canh Sat jeep came up behind the Lambretta and then pulled out suddenly. A policeman motioned the Lambretta to the curb and when it stopped two

more policemen with M-3 submachine guns hanging care-
lessly from web straps around their necks got out of the jeep
and surrounded the Lambretta. The driver of the jeep
stayed in the vehicle, but the policeman who had motioned
the Lambretta driver to stop began checking the operator's
documents. They talked back and forth while the muzzle of
one submachine gun wavered by only inches from Knox's
ear, and the Vietnamese women covered their faces with the
hems of their *ao dais* and the Army sergeant sat impassively.

The policeman examined one of the thin plastic-bound
documents, then another, arguing with the driver all the
while. He grasped the driver by one arm and motioned toward the Canh Sat jeep. The driver pulled his arm away.
The policemen with submachine guns pivoted them at the
Lambretta driver. He stopped and slowly took out a worn
leather purse. He counted out some piastre bills. The policeman took them and recounted them, then returned the
Lambretta driver's documents. The policemen got into
their jeep and pulled back into the flow of traffic.

One of the women asked the driver something and he answered angrily. "A little bit of squeeze," the sergeant said.

"Tax," Knox said. "He no have right pafer."

"Sorry 'bout that," the sergeant said.

Knox watched the lights coming on in the stores on either
side of the street and knew (felt, rather like a swift and un-
looked-for blow to the belly) that there was corruption in
just looking at evil. He got out at the intersection of Cong
Ly with Phan dinh Phung and walked the four long blocks
to his house. He was very tired now and carried his suitcase
clumsily. It banged against his heels and once almost
tripped him. When he reached the villa, he threw it into a
corner of the living room. Rosette had been there. Some
new fish were swimming in the aquarium and flowers were
dropping petals from a new vase on the table. Knox

checked the refrigerator for something to eat, but the electricity had been off and the food had spoiled into one putrid mass of mold. So he turned on the overhead fan as well as the air conditioner and sat under the fan and ate tomato soup straight from the can and afterward went to bed.

Saigon Again

I

KNOX WENT to the office late the next morning and made his report to Mister Balfour. Sitting quietly in the room full of unseen presences, like held breath. As far as he knew, he had accomplished no definite objective, but for some obscure reason Mister Balfour seemed pleased, perhaps because Knox had returned safely.

"That's fine," Mister Balfour said when Knox finished. He switched his attention to other things. "Give me a memo on it, turn any film you took over to the photo lab for developing and let me see anything you think is worthwhile. For your information, a train was ambushed ten clicks south of Da Lat yesterday. The VC blew up the entire train and cut the track in three places. Your report on track conditions will be academic, but make it anyway. In the standard number of copies." Mister Balfour bent to his perpetual task of sorting through the papers piled on his desk, exercising his penchant for wanting things right, not necessarily useful.

Knox knew he had been dismissed. He was annoyed because Mister Balfour did not exhibit any appreciation for the hardships he believed he had endured.

Not that he had been given a chance to relate any of them. But he was learning not to let his anger or annoyance show. So he left and closed the door very quietly. Mr. Khiem was in his office under his small conical shaft of light, and as usual he got up and bowed formally. And as usual Knox did not acknowledge the bow but passed without looking at the Vietnamese.

That afternoon he went downtown with B.D. and ordered two pairs of Saigon fatigues, much to B.D.'s disgust. They went to a tailor shop on Tu Do just down the street from the Caravelle, where Knox was measured by a bearded Indian tailor complete with dirty turban who whispered that he could have a discount if he wanted to pay in US green. But Knox ignored him, and paid a deposit in piastres after selecting the colors and material and making sure both sets would have a pocket on the left sleeve.

They went out of the tailor shop and walked up Tu Do toward the Constituent Assembly. Small children were hawking shoe shines or begging for money outside bars, feeling their pockets for coins as they passed, children already old and sharp eyed. B.D. kept saying *"di di"* and brushing them off. After a while the children gave up on them and went back to their stations in front of the bars to patrol vigilantly for the next American passer-by.

"Let's have a beer," B.D. said.

"Good," Knox said. "I'll buy."

They stopped at the Continental Palace and took a table at the edge of the verandah. The waiter came and they ordered Ba-me-ba. They drank their beer and watched the pedestrian traffic of whores and pimps and beggars and war cripples and the double amputee in a dirty fatigue shirt and a sailor hat who pushed himself along on a little cart with old roller skates for casters.

Then someone called B.D.'s name and Knox looked around and saw a group of three people coming up the low steps from the street. B.D.'s name was called again, and he

got up, agilely for all his bulk, and shook hands with a tall
bald American in slacks and a short-sleeved shirt. Knox got
up, too, and B.D. introduced the man as Calvin Davies, a
pilot for Continental Air Charter. The other two men were
wearing the short-sleeved tropical uniform with the
rounded collars of Air Force officers, with badges and trappings of rank and presumed accomplishments above their
left breast pockets. The one with the most ribbons sat down
in a chair he pulled over from the next table and introduced
himself as Captain True. He had a handsome scar which
puckered the skin of his forehead into a tight perpetual appearance of studiousness. He also had a broken tooth which
showed whenever he smiled or laughed. The other man did
not have as many ribbons and he needed a shave badly. His
uniform was rumpled and his aviation badge was different
from True's. His name was Loescher and he never looked
at anyone directly, but always at a point somewhere below
the chin.

"What do you chaps do for a living?" True asked.

"We work at the Embassy," B.D. said.

"I get it. You work for the Agency and do cloak-and-dag-
ger stuff."

"You're good at guessing games."

"No guesswork involved. Calvin wouldn't know you if
you were buried somewhere just shuffling papers." True
was grinning. His broken tooth was showing and he was
having difficulty in focusing his eyes. But he still purposely
avoided looking at Knox. He slapped a hand on the table.
"Where's our goddamn drinks? We've been here five whole
minutes and the fuckers haven't brought our drinks."

"You haven't ordered anything yet," B.D. said.

Some people sitting several tables away turned and
looked at True. A waiter hurried up, his sandals slapping

against the soles of his feet. "Bring up the Scotch, papa-san, and jiggle your dick. We're thirsty."

Then the two Air Force captains began talking earnestly between themselves. B.D. glared at them with faint hostility. "Get two fliers together and they'll start trying to outlie each other with their war stories."

"Come off it, B.D.," Davies said. "They're not that bad. True was an F four pilot and Loescher was his navigator for a while."

B.D. grunted. The waiter hurried up with their drinks. Davies paid for them and raised his glass to B.D. "Prosit."

"Prosit," B.D. said.

The two fliers were singing, "Strafe the town and kill the people, shoot the children as they run . . ." but people at other tables were really looking at them now, and Davies made them stop.

"You still changing green?" B.D. said.

"You know better than to ask that, B.D. I wouldn't tell you even if I were," said Davies.

"You'd better stay out of the market. I saved your ass last time, but if it happens again J. H. Christ Himself and all the angels can't help you."

"Let's have dinner here, B.D.; for old time's sake. I'm not hurting for coin. Come on, join me. I've got to get these two sobered up enough to get them back to Tan son Nhut."

"Okay, this place's as good as another." B.D. signaled their waiter and told him they wanted a table in the dining room. The waiter nodded and returned in five minutes to lead them to a table in the dining room. In the meantime they all had had another drink.

Their table was next to one of the curtained-off banquet rooms and they had hardly ordered dinner before a group of Vietnamese men in business suits filed into the curtained room. Someone opened the drapes because of the heat and they could see that the Saigon chapter of the Rotary Club was holding a meeting.

A waiter served their rolls and butter. One of the Vietnamese in the banquet room touched the tone arm of an old French phonograph to a record. All the members of the Rotary Club were standing. B.D. heard the first notes of the music and stood up.

"What the hell are you doing?" True said.

B.D. flushed dull red at the base of his neck and the large freckles there stood out vividly. He said nothing, but remained standing until the music ended.

"You do that every time the ginks play some music?" Loescher asked.

B.D. hawked and cleared his throat. The way he always did when he was pregnant with phlegm or an idea. But all he said was, "You're drunk."

Loescher giggled.

Davies changed the subject. "Why aren't there any grenade screens around this place? This would make a damn fine target for some VC sapper squad."

"Don't worry about it," B.D. said. "The Palace pays VC protection tax. You're as safe here as in your own house."

The dinner was the equivalent of the meal Knox had eaten at the Quilliam Tell. True excused himself and vanished in the direction of the washroom. He was gone a long time. They ate a custard with sherry sauce and drank a cup of gritty French coffee. True still had not appeared. Davies got up finally and went to the bathroom. He was back in a moment and bent over to whisper urgently in B.D.'s ear.

"You've got to give me a hand. True's in the latrine with his head stuck in the john. He's puked up his guts."

"Put him in a taxi and point him toward Tan son Nhut."

"He'd never make it, not in the shape he's in."

"Screw him. It's his fault for not being able to hold his liquor. The big brave fighter jock who can't hold his Scotch. You weren't slowing him down any." B.D.'s nostrils were pinched and the pupils of his eyes were dilated despite the intensity of the light.

"Shit, B.D. I wouldn't leave you like this. Give the guys a break. Help me out just this once and I'll — "

"Don't do me any favors. Just keep these crapheads out of my way." B.D. motioned to Knox. "Make yourself useful. Get the one out of the john and walk him up the street toward the cathedral." He heaved his bulk out of the chair. Then to Davies: "I'm doing this for you, not your goddamn friends."

Knox went to the washroom. The small Vietnamese attendant was squatting beside True and holding a wet towel to his neck. True was sitting on the floor with his chin resting on the edge of the urinal. His shoulders heaved and his cheeks pursed as he tried to vomit, but nothing came up. Everything he had recently eaten or drunk reeked in the urinal or spotted the front of his uniform.

Knox pulled True to his feet with some difficulty. The attendant wiped at the front of True's shirt but only succeeded in distributing the vomit over his collection of ribbons. Knox gave him a few piastres and the attendant opened the door for them.

Calvin Davies met him in the hallway. He was supporting Loescher by the arm. They walked their charges down the side stairs and started up the sidewalk past the travel bureau and on toward the cathedral. True kept stumbling on the broken sidewalk. He was almost a dead weight. Knox was perspiring heavily before they had gone a hundred yards.

They were almost to John F. Kennedy Square when a black Embassy station wagon slid up behind them. B.D. got out of the right front seat and opened a rear door. "Get them inside."

"It took you long enough," Davies said.

"Bitch, bitch, bitch. I got some transportation, didn't I?"

"Yeah, I didn't mean to sound ungrateful. Come on. Let's get them to Tan son Nhut."

True was rousing. He sang a few bars of "Mu Ghia Pass" to the tune of a song from *West Side Story*. "Mu Ghia, Mu Ghia, I just hit a pass named Mu Gh — ia." Then Knox put a hand over True's mouth and the song trailed away into a gurgle. A jeep of Army MPs was passing. The night sky was pocked by the eerie yellow illumination of parachute flares. They could hear the dull crump of artillery fire from across the Saigon River. True hiccupped and began to take more interest in his surroundings. Knox pushed True into the front seat and got in beside him. B.D., Davies and Loescher got into the back. Men grinned and his teeth flashed dull gold from the light of the instrument panel.

"Where you go, Ong Knox?"

"Tan son Nhut," Knox said.

II

Mister Balfour was wiping his glasses. His head was bent over his desk and he kept moving the handkerchief around and around the lenses. He was taking much longer than necessary. All chairs except his had been removed from the office. As a consequence they were standing in front of his desk. Knox could sense that B.D. was desperate for a cigarette. His hand half lifted toward his shirt pocket several times, but each time Mister Balfour stopped polishing his glasses until B.D. dropped his hand.

Finally Mister Balfour had the glasses as clean as he

wanted, or perhaps he had grown tired of the game. He
slipped the temples over his ears and adjusted them meticulously. "Why did you have to call an Embassy car?" he
said finally.

"They didn't know we were agents."

"The hell they didn't. The fact that Davies knew you was
proof enough. And they weren't drunk enough to forget
they were in an Embassy car. And when that frapping general at Seventh Air Force called the Ambassador this morning he right away bucked it down to me. For chrissakes,
next time you go out drinking use a contract car, or take a
taxi."

"There wouldn't have been room for all of us in a taxi,"
B.D. said.

"That MP patrol was right in stopping you and taking
you out to the base. Bar hopping in an Embassy car. Is
that being very professional? What would happen to you if
word of this got back to Mr. Helms?" Mister Balfour's telephone rang and he answered it. He listened intently for a
moment and wiped his forehead with a clean handkerchief
he took from a desk drawer. "Don't bother me with it over
the phone," he said abruptly. "Write it out and let me have
it in an IIR." He paused and glared once more at B.D., who
had gotten the cigarette pack out of his shirt pocket. B.D.
put it back. Mister Balfour returned to the telephone. "I
want everything about the elections written out in an IIR."
He dropped the receiver on the cradle.

"Trouble," Knox said. Hopefully.

"Of a sort. The Buddhists are threatening some difficul-
ties for the government during the elections. Possibly some
riots and demonstrations before the campaigning gets
started." Mister Balfour shook his head. "We have to watch
the Buddhists closely. It's organized superstition and there's
nothing worse. Next thing you know they'll have mobs in

the streets and then a full-scale rebellion. Mobs lead to that sort of thing, you know."

Mister Balfour leaned back thoughtfully and formed a bridge with his fingers. Because he knew the dictionary terms for things he was satisfied, not understanding they were just meaningless measured words because the diction- ary meanings were hiding him from the full extent of his ig- norance. But none of them knew that then, and B.D. only suspected it. Mister Balfour shook his head slowly. "Super- stitions, superstitions. Now back to you two. The damage's done. There's no crying over it now. You both exhibited a remarkable lack of prudence. Especially you, Knox. Your father would never understand how you could become involved in such a thing."

"Are you going to tell him, sir?"

"No. I've thought about it. I can see no reason to. I can't see any reason not to, either. He wrote me and asked me to keep an eye on you. Did you know that?"

"I've written to him. It must be that the mails are slow."

"You both have to watch things like this. The Air Force doesn't like to have their officers picked up for drunkenness. Your friends' asses have been properly singed by now. But don't worry about yourselves. I'll paper things over at the Em- bassy. I've got to go to the Annex this morning, and I'll take care of it then. It's just too bad it was an Embassy car. Otherwise we could have disavowed the whole incident. It gives us a bad image." Mister Balfour dismissed them.

B.D. smoked a cigarette between the time they were out- side Mister Balfour's office door and the time it took to walk to B.D.'s office. He slumped in his chair and drank ice water straight from the pitcher until the sweat showed dark through his shirt. He lit another cigarette and looked at Knox through the smoke. "Go and sin no more."

Knox ignored him and picked up an IIR. "This is the

tenth IIR I've seen this month saying the VC are going to launch an attack on Binh Thuy Air Base during the next full moon. Don't you think this is all a bit much?"

"Don't worry about it. Just get it looking good and send it out. At least we've got our ass covered. If you predict it long enough when it really happens you've got something in file to drag out and say to all and sundry, 'Haw, mother-fucker, I told you so.'"

"It's a waste."

"Like I say, every rule is its own reward. Never mind the facts, give them the straight trivia."

III

Knox sought out the Gypsy Bar. The day had been tense with the effort of appearing to do everything while actually doing nothing. Another day when form had been the arbiter of importance and substance was secondary. He had worked hard to maintain the appearance of working hard, and as a consequence was tired. B.D. had pointed out just before Knox left the office that Americans like bustle and the thrill of hurrying because they think they are accomplishing something if they just appear busy. For if anything happens it is essential to do something. Anything. B.D. refused to rush, though he was expert in appearing to be busy, too. And Knox had copied Mister Balfour's tautological stratagem of piling his desk with papers.

He had gotten his Saigon fatigues that noon. It had taken less than a day for the tailor to make them, and one or two of the seams showed that. But the fabric was cool and slippery on his skin, welcome in the heat. He also wore a pair of Air Force issue sunglasses stolen from the Saigon docks and purchased at a street corner for less than it cost the manufacturer to make the frames.

Knox walked into the dim hot cave that was the Gypsy Bar and saw Rosette at a table. She was with Calvin Davies, True, and another bargirl he had seen in the Gypsy. They looked up in surprise. Except True. He was also wearing a pair of Air Force sunglasses and they masked any surprise he may have shown. Knox drew up a plastic-bottomed chair and sat down. The five of them effectively blocked the narrow space between the wall and the bar and if someone had come in and wanted to go to the end of the bar Knox would have had to have moved. But it was still early and it would be perhaps thirty minutes before the first soldier would find his way to the high-priced beer and fleshy delights of the Gypsy Bar. The girls were already waiting. They never stopped waiting. Clustered in small groups around the door, or patiently playing tick tack toe or seven-card gin at the bar; thin bodies moving continuously inside their scant garments with the awkward and voluptuous purposelessness of the young. They scrutinized Knox with the savage dead lust of calculation, but he was marked as Rosette's, and they left him alone.

Rosette made a studied casualness of her nonchalance as they shook hands around. "This is my girl, Mai," True said. "I call her the cuntess." He laughed as if he had said something funny. Very, very funny. Mai laughed too.

"You come here very often?" Knox said.

"Every time I'm in town. Best beer in Saigon."

"It's the same as anyplace else."

"Rosette and I are old friends," Davis said. "I'd heard she had a patron now. I had no idea it would be you. Hope you don't mind if I just talk to her."

"Any reason I should?"

"Actually, we're discussing a purely business transaction.

Rosette says I have to have your blessing before we do anything. My guess is that you got her cherry so she's committed to you. Over here women come in sealed bottles if they want to marry well. You've given her no choice but to have you as a patron."

Knox ignored most of what Davies said. "What sort of arrangement did you have in mind?"

"Well now, I'm not certain we can discuss it fully. Perhaps we should discuss it someplace else."

"You talk okay here," Mai said. "Gypsy plenty safe. No buddy hear you." She and True were holding hands under the table. True had two empty Ballantine cans in front of him.

"All right. I'll take a chance. In a general way. I'd still like to talk to you later." A soldier came in and a bargirl detached herself from the group around the door and snared him. She reminded Knox of a limpet. He started to get up to allow the soldier to pass, but the soldier took a seat close to the door.

Davies lowered his voice. "I really think we'd be better off talking somewhere else." He inclined his head slightly toward the soldier.

"Oh come on, Calvin, spit it out." From his slurred tones it was evident True had had more than two beers.

"Rosette and I engaged in a little moneychanging deal. Beginning about six months ago. Before that I was dealing with the Indians on Tu Do and a couple of Chinese in Cholon. But I got caught. The Indians have a passion for records, and the Army CID pulled a raid on one of the tailor shops and got hold of a list with my name on it. They turned it over to CAS, and if your fat friend Drummond hadn't spoken up for me my ass would have been grass."

"How does this concern me?"

"Well, it's like this. Rosette has some good contacts in the market. I've been giving her some green every now and

along and she's been buying MPC. But since you came on
the scene as her patron I've got to clue you in on the deal or
she won't continue. That's the way these Vietnamese
broads are."

"What you're doing is illegal, of course."

"No more than a lot of things other people, big people,
not small fry like me, are doing. And I know you won't report me."

"What says I won't?"

"I say you won't. You've already changed money here.
For all I or CAS know you may have changed it on the
street as well. At least that's how CAS would look at it.
You're living in a villa where you're paying a lot more than
the lease says. Besides, if you can get a source of green,
there's a percentage in it for you."

Knox looked at Rosette and she lowered her eyes and
toyed with the beetle watch on the chain around her neck.

Davies saw where he was looking. "Rosette didn't tell
me. I got my information from papa-san. He's got your
name in a book. You'd better pray this place doesn't get
raided. But I don't want you to think I'm threatening you."

"I don't think you're threatening me in the least." Knox
gave off the insipid odor of superiority. "Everybody seems
to be changing money. It's fashionable from what I've seen.
It only involves a local law, and laws can change."

The soldier had drunk one beer and departed. The bargirl had pouted and tried to keep him at the Gypsy, but it
was all pretense. True was trying clandestinely but obviously to see up the girl's skirt.

"The gutless wonder," True said. Everyone at the table
looked at him.

"How do you think the elections are going to go?" Davies
said. He said it deliberately, to change the conversation.

Both he and Knox were adept at changing topics of conversation.

"Your guess is as good as mine," Knox said.

"Come on. It's your business to know. It looks like Thieu and Ky are sure winners."

"How did Ky let himself get talked into second place?" True said. "It should be the other way around."

"I saw one report on that. It seems there was a big meeting of all the people with any say in the government, and Ky was insisting that Thieu run, so everybody could protest and say Ky was the only one who could win, so he could accept by acclamation. He was trying to create a little face, and of course Thieu was insisting that Ky was the only one to run for the first spot, and they were drinking a lot. It finally broke down into a crying match between Thieu and Ky, and when Ky got up on the table and insisted that Thieu run, Thieu accepted and Ky found he couldn't back down without losing a lot of face. He didn't want it that way, but there were too many people present."

"He let his mouth overload his ass," True said.

"It's the other way around," Davies said.

"Ky has a pretty snatch for a wife," True said.

"Yes," Davies said. "That's an asset if he were running for office in the States. Americans like to see a politician with a pretty wife. Makes them think he's honest."

Rosette grimaced. "She dinky dau. We work Butterfly Bar together. She bargirl just same me. Now she Missus Ky she no even talk old friends."

"Thieu and Ky will probably sweep the elections. They'll have enough ballots ready to be switched if the voting starts to go the other way."

"That's not what the poll watchers are saying."

"Jesus Christ, you mean that bunch of politicians and

wienies they're bringing in to watch the polls? Hell, they don't even know the language, or the slick ways these people have of seeming to do something when they're doing exactly the opposite." Davies paused to sip his beer. "The Vietnamese government has a vested interest in keeping this war going because of the foreign aid. All the big generals and politicians are socking away plenty of coin. This war's going to go on for a long time."

"Maybe the Vietnamese will send poll watchers to the States next year." True said. The bargirl, Mai, had gotten him another beer.

"I've seen some of the tricks the Embassy's pulled. We can't let anyone but Thieu and Ky win. No matter what Washington says about free determination. We're backing Thieu and Ky and every Vietnamese knows it, plain as a wart on your dick."

"Oh God," True said. "How did we ever get into this philosophical shit? This crud makes me thirsty."

"You're drunk," Davies said.

"No, but I'm getting there. Just living up to my reputation as a fighter pilot."

Mai leaned over and nibbled at his ear. True drew away. "Stop that, cuntess."

"You aren't a fighter pilot anymore," Davies said.

"Once a fighter pilot always a fighter pilot. One hand on the throttle, the other on my cock." Both bargirls giggled and covered their mouths with their hands.

"Better quit while you're ahead and remember last night," Davies said. He reached over and took the beer can away from True. "You've had enough."

He turned to Knox. "So, is it a deal? I can go ahead with Rosette in our little business. And you see if you can't figure out a way to get in on the action."

"What about True?"

"What *about* me?" said True.

"Are you sure he won't be talking about your changing money?"

"Hell, he's not interested about anything but flying, drinking and screwing. He changes green, too, like anybody else when he gets short."

"Damn right," True said. "It's in the manuals. And I don't want to go back to the base. I'm having fun right here." He tried to fix his gaze on Mai, but it wavered. "How about it, cuntess, you gonna show me the action? You got a place I can stay, and not any two-bit short-time pad, either."

"This friend Rosette have beaucoup place. Maybe he let you stay."

"Is that so? How about putting me up for a day? I promise not to puke on your rug."

"Yeah, why not?" Davies said. "He's not used to Saigon, and I can't be hauling him around from Tan son Nhut and back every day."

Knox hesitated. True held out his hand, palm upward. "I got no place to go, friend. Davies has had a bellyful of hauling me around."

"Okay. I can do it for a day or two."

"Good." Davies went to the bar and paid for all the drinks. He returned to the table and shook hands with Knox. "Find yourself some green and play the game with us."

True wanted to lie down for a while. He was sitting with both hands planted firmly on the table. Knox got True outside and hailed a taxi.

"I hate this fucking place," True said. He tapped the taxi driver on the shoulder. "Vietnam sucks." The driver scowled and shook his head quickly from side to side. He was old and wizened and had no teeth.

"He doesn't understand English," Knox said.

"He understands that Vietnam sucks." True sat back on the faded seat. It gave off a faint aurora of dust motes which danced briefly in the air.

"Maybe you ought to go back to the States and see what the rest of the world's like."

"Not me. They've got hippies and demonstrations back there. I'm safer over here."

"Well, what is it about free love and communes and not bathing that you don't like?"

"I really can't say. I don't know what it's all about, but I don't like it anyway." True looked dreamily out the window of the cab at a Vietnamese girl on a Solex. Her conical hat was tied under her chin with a wide satin ribbon and they could not see her face for the shade, but the tail of her *ao dai* was clipped to the back of her Solex and she looked as graceful as a moth. And just as fragile. "Man, that Mai is something else. I bet she can do more tricks on an eight-inch dick than a monkey on a thousand-foot vine."

Kiting

KNOX SENT two checks for $1000 each drawn on his State-side account to two fraternity brothers in Denver, and they sent him $2000 in currency of large denominations through the APO mails. He gave the money to Rosette and she changed it with a Chinaman in Cholon for $3400 in MPC. Knox bought a money order from the Bank of America branch in downtown Saigon and mailed the money order to his bank for deposit. He sent two more checks to his fraternity brothers. One of them wrote and asked why he needed so much money and Knox replied that he had difficulty in cashing personal checks in Vietnam. His fraternity brother was satisfied and Knox said he would give him ten dollars for every check the fraternity brother cashed to cover the bother of mailing and going to the bank. But by all means to enclose the bills in several folds of writing paper so no mail clerk would guess what was inside.

He now had a source of green and proceeded to use it. Knox bought a car with all the optional equipment he could think of through a factory representative at a Tan son Nhut Exchange. He paid the full price of $4800 in MPC. Two weeks later he wrote the manufacturer and requested them to cancel his order because he was going to be in Vietnam longer than he had previously thought. He asked the company to deposit the purchase price in his

Stateside account. In due course he got a letter from the car manufacturer stating that a refund had been made, and that they hoped they would have the opportunity of doing business with him again. Shortly thereafter, his bank sent him a deposit slip for the full $4800. So he learned and became a party to the machinations, subtleties and devious methods of obtaining green and kiting it. With never a thought as to where the money was going or what it would be used to finance; or if he thought of it at all, he considered it less than the shadow of a cigarette ash.

Knox did not need the money, but he kept cashing checks through his fraternity brothers and kiting it for green through Rosette because once he saw how easy it was he had no real reason to stop, nor even a desire to. His one account soon had over $10,000 in it, so he opened another account in a different bank, in California this time, and used his name without a middle initial. Then he started on another set of friends, using them unscrupulously to send him more green. Because it was now more like a game than anything else. Playing with it as he had played with his marriage. The money was a symbol of something; like cards, a diversion. Something with assigned values played under arbitrary rules. Wanting the money as he had wanted his wife, because the thing looked good and the others would envy him for having it. Not that he could tell anyone about the money, or how he accrued it, but if people knew he had the money they would be envious, and how he obtained it would not really matter.

Each negotiation enmeshed him deeper in the business of profiteering during a war. Davies called him several times from the airport when he flew in from out-of-country trips. Knox met him at Tan son Nhut, where Davies gave him envelopes of money which he passed to Rosette. Knox took a percentage of it, too, because Rosette was taking a percentage just as Davies knew Knox was taking a percentage. For it was all very much expected and he regarded it as no more than his just due and recompense for the risk involved, though there really was no risk, and they all knew that, too.

The daily routine of rewriting IIRs was as tedious as ever and he sought relief in Rosette. He saw several small pieces of information in IIRs concerning low-level Viet Cong agents in Saigon that CAS was vetting for possible penetration. Most of the Viet Cong agents were very small operatives, only a few cadre were identified, and CAS was content to leave them alone in hopes they could be vetted and eventually doubled. But Knox by chance let slip some otherwise innocuous remark when True was staying with him, and Rosette turned a low-level VC agent's name over to the National Police. The National Police arrested the man, questioned him and duly certified him as an actual Viet Cong sapper. Rosette got two thousand piastres for denouncing the man. She pumped Knox for more names, and he gave them to her, unwittingly at first; then he caught on and still furnished her names, identification card numbers and addresses because he saw nothing wrong with it. Besides, these people were already marked as Viet Cong and someone would turn them in sooner or later.

Rosette quit the Gypsy Bar and was living with Knox. She bragged to her friends that Knox was the actual head of American intelligence in Saigon, and as his mistress she had a certain amount of position to maintain. He gave her money from time to time. He did not know at first what she did with the money, and assumed she sent some of it to the mother and sister she sometimes talked about but he never expected to see. She had the percentage she got from changing green with the Chinese, and the rewards for the denouncements. Rosette had a French passport, too, and was not dependent upon the eleemosynary patronage of others for her support.

She was buying rice and hoarding it. She bought the fine long-grained rice that came from Thailand and Okinawa when she could get it, and the hard-kerneled IR-8 which was just starting to be grown in quantity through the assistance of the USAID advisers. She bought the AID rice from Texas and Louisiana which was stolen from the docks, and when she exhausted her money, she asked Knox for more.

She stored the rice in the spare bedroom until the bed had to be moved against the wall near the door and the windows were blocked. The bathroom in that bedroom had already been filled, as had the kitchen. Rosette built a small lean-to against the side of the villa from beer tins and stolen two-by-fours. The bartender from the Gypsy Bar built it in the early mornings when Knox was at the office because she was afraid to trust anyone else. Whenever the price of rice climbed, she waited until it reached a certain point, then she sold. When the prices fell she bought. Usually the government stepped in when the prices inflated too quickly, but she was remarkably astute in gauging the tenor of the market. She had to sell short only once when the government clamped a price ceiling on rice. The price had been higher the week before so she had to sell at the official price because it was election week and she was afraid someone would denounce her as a profiteer if she sold higher.

Rosette speculated in rice and skimmed a percentage from the money she took to Cholon in a plain market bag and denounced Viet Cong sympathizers impartially to the vast discomfort of the sympathizers and CAS. While she became more and more Knox's mistress and fairly wealthy in her own right. Each the plaything of the other. He was spending more time with her than he spent at the office on most days, but no one at CAS took much notice when he came in late or left early or stayed away for an extra long lunch break. For others were doing this also. And he, for his part, took this as part of his birthright as he did most things, and never repaid the debt. Each said he loved the other because it seemed to fit the time and the occasion. They knew it was not true, but they believed it anyway because they wanted to, and that was all it took. Deception was relatively simple.

For Knox had gone to school, done all the things children did, and when he was bigger had done all the things big kids had done; he was inert, passive, acted upon rather than acting — reacting rather. Not knowing what was happening inside him, or whether he was happy or sad; not knowing what he wanted, though he had his reasons (unknown to him) for doing what he did. While Rosette, bemused and hesitant, stood trying to determine her own mind in the best way, the most lucrative, through the strange loveless oscillation between instinct and calculation, avarice and a strange kind of caring.

True was coming to Saigon every chance he got. To see Mai. Though he still said that "dumb Vietnamese" was redundant. They went to the big exchange at Cholon and bought a refrigerator for Knox, a Sanyo, and a very small one, to replace the one that had come with the villa but which no longer worked. The refrigerator bulked large in its packing crate and they had to bring it back to the villa in a cyclo.

They returned and bought other things, too. With the money Knox was making in the currency market and the ration cards True had. Knox had no compunction about asking how. He borrowed an Embassy car to transport the television set, the tape recorder, the amplifier and the liquor. Feeling even righteous about it because at least he was being open, and being open was the best way of escaping detection.

Knox bought a Mini-Moke through his currency manipulations. Rosette told him of a Chinese who did not have enough MPC to buy some green, so Knox told her to drive a hard bargain and he got the Mini-Moke. He and True drove it around Saigon one Sunday, and they had great expectations of it, but it was stolen the next day. He had locked the steering wheel but it was so light and so small that someone loaded it into a truck after pushing it out of the alley. He suspected the former owner, but Rosette could not find the man again.

Rosette brought a fortuneteller to the villa the week after the elections to buy rice. The fortuneteller was visibly upset when he saw the house. He began pacing the length of the courtyard and stopped to make some measurements on the alley walls with his hands from time to time. It was a Sunday again, the Sunday after the Mini-Moke drive through Saigon, and Knox was in the living room, reading the *Stars and Stripes*. He came out and asked Rosette what the old man was doing.

"He a soothsayer," Rosette said. "He say house bad location."

"Tell him to get bent."

"He beaucoup soothsayer. He give advice all time General Khanh."

"General Khanh lost out to somebody two years ago."

"General Khanh no listen soothsayer. It his responsible he no listen." Rosette talked to the soothsayer and he replied in Mandarin Vietnamese, making graphic sweeping movements with his hands as he talked. He made several stabbing motions with a forefinger toward his heart and forehead. His forefinger was tipped with a long yellow nail which curved like a talon on some strange wizened bird. "Soothsayer tell this house end of street. Street point like knife to house. This much bad."

"He beaucoup sou you, Rosette."

Rosette caught him by the arm as he turned to go back into the house. "Old man know. He have third eye."

Knox shrugged off her hand.

"He have cards show you." Rosette motioned to the old man and he squatted at the edge of the tile porch. He very patiently wiped the tiles in front of him clear of dust and shuffled a frayed deck of tarot cards. He held them close to his wispy beard and intoned a chant, threw them down and spread them. The old man tapped the backs of the cards with two coins. He shuffled the deck again and flipped a card out of the center. Queen of hearts. He held the deck of cards toward Knox.

"Take card please."

Knox reached out and riffled through the deck, selected a card and turned it over. Two of spades. The soothsayer smoothed a patch of dirt beside him and drew a large heart in the dirt with a straight line through the lower tip. The line was parallel with the alley and he tipped the straight line with an arrowhead drawn in the shape of a spade.

Rosette was biting her lower lip. "Street is knife. Draw bad luck."

Knox shook his head. "I'm not moving, and even if we could find a better place I'm not moving all that rice." He went inside and turned on the air conditioner despite the lingering coolness of the morning. He heard Rosette and the soothsayer talking outside, and after a while the soothsayer went away.

But an hour later he returned. He was accompanied by a small boy who carried a large mirror which had been poorly silvered. The soothsayer carried a hammer and a small sack of nails. He carefully measured a spot on the outside wall facing the alley and drove in a nail. Several chunks of mortar fell out of the wall and broke into minute fragments. He hung the mirror and made several small adjustments until he was satisfied. The fortuneteller looked at the mirror from different angles and nodded to Rosette. Rosette gave him some folded piastre notes and two sacks of Thai rice. The boy carried one sack with difficulty, but the old man slung the other fifty-kilo sack over his shoulder and carried it down the alley without faltering. Knox and Rosette followed. The soothsayer and the boy put the rice in a three-wheeled bicycle cart parked against the curbing at the entrance to the alley. The soothsayer crouched in the front and the boy got on the bicycle seat and slowly pedaled away.

Knox turned. Sunlight reflected off the mirror and struck him full in the eyes, blinding him.

Rosette was obviously pleased with herself. "Mirror send back evil come from street. Things numba one."

"You were had," Knox said, and went back to finish the *Stars and Stripes*.

That was not the only time Knox saw the old fortuneteller. He saw him at the CAS office the following Wednesday. He could not find B.D. to ask his advice on an IIR, but another agent told him B.D. was in an interview room. Knox entered without knocking and found the old soothsayer in the room with B.D. and Mr. Khiem. The soothsayer did not show any recognition.

"You might as well come in," B.D. said. "Sit down and learn something."

"What's this guy doing here?"

"Sit down and keep quiet. He's on the payroll."

Khiem was interpreting questions B.D. asked and translating the fortuneteller's replies. They were discussing prominent Vietnamese politicians. The soothsayer was repeating questions these people had asked him, and also the replies he had given. B.D. listened intently and scribbled on a note pad whenever the soothsayer said something he considered important. The fortuneteller was reciting almost the entire list of cabinet figures so far named by the newly formed Thieu government.

It took him a long time to finish and when he did B.D. gave him a list of responses he was to make if these people approached him again. B.D. put an envelope on the edge of the desk, and the soothsayer very carefully counted the money. He signed a receipt B.D. held out to him. The soothsayer bowed to B.D. and left the room with Mr. Khiem.

"What's all this?"

B.D. worked over the pad for a while without looking up. "Trying to influence Vietnamese policy," he said finally. "Most Viets, Catholics or Buddhists or whatever, believe in these mumbo-jumbo artists. That old fossil is one of the best, or at least one of the most influential. He tells us what important people ask him — for a price of course. A very high price, because he's fairly honest. And we tell him what to tell these very important clients if they pose certain questions."

"Such as how to prosecute the war and how to get along with us Americans."

"Precisely."

"It's all a crock of shit."

"Such language," B.D. said. "You've fallen among bad companions. Maybe it's shit plain and simple, but not to these people. The inauguration was postponed several times because Thieu wanted the stars to be right. That's just a for instance. This old goat has some good prophecies on occasion. So many they have to be more than guesses. He said the old

Embassy was going to have a bad accident because it faced away from the river. A bad omen. The old Embassy took a pasting from a Charlie sapper squad last year. He's predicted other bad things, like for Gia Long Palace. Seems the gatehouse is too far from the main building and bad spirits can enter. The palace was mortared the night Humphrey was there. He's right just enough to keep you listening."

"So CAS uses him to get through to the politicians."

"And the generals. Don't leave out the generals. They're old hands at consulting soothsayers. Always wanting to know who's plotting against them; who's plotting against whom, and who's got the best scheme with the greatest chance of success. They're probably the old man's best customers."

"Which politician does he trust the most?" Knox asked.

"The one who doesn't ask his advice," B.D. said.

Street Children

B.D. NEEDED some razor blades and an excuse to get out of
the office. He and Knox could have walked to the Brinks
Exchange, but that was too close, and they both wanted to
escape the maddening tedium of the IIR rewrite as long as
possible, some respite from the insular CAS protected from
itself by its musty cocoon of regulations. They signed out
an Embassy jeep and drove to the main Army Exchange in
Cholon via Hong thap Tu and Hung Vuong with a detour
through the central market so they would not arrive before
opening time. The sun was not yet high so the morning was
still cool when they arrived at the compound. B.D. drove
hopefully around the compound, but all the parking places
close in were taken. They had to park a block away under
the tall graceful trees with vehicle-scarred sides, close to the
Cholon Cathedral, where the Diem brothers had sought refuge after the November coup, and from which they had
been removed by promise of amnesty and armored car. But
their captors had taken the thoughtful precaution of relieving them of their lives lest they prove an embarrassment to
subsequent regimes to sit in Gia Long Palace.

B.D. parked the jeep and secured the wheel. Fighting off
the onslaught of urchins who offered to watch the jeep for
ten piastres, and the old women in dirty pantaloons wanting
to sell them toy dolls dressed in miniature *ao dais* in brightly

colored shoe boxes; past the beggars and the taxi drivers who would take you to Tan son Nhut for one hundred piastres, in advance. Past all these people without really seeing them and into the restless mass of GIs and RMK civilians, after showing their passes to the MP at the gate. Knox wandered by the stacks of good luggage, refrigerators, television sets, radios, tape recorders, liquors, cased beer, soft drinks, jewelry, fur coats and hair spray. Which were purchased by the soldiers, the airmen, the civilians of half a dozen different countries, and some of which would find its way to the black market the day it was bought to be placed beside comparable merchandise stolen from the docks and open storage bays.

B.D. could not find the razor blades he wanted, and Knox bought only a container of washing powder for his housekeeper. They left quickly and got out of the jostling crowd in the air-conditioned buildings. B.D. bought a milk shake at the snack bar just inside the gate and drank it all before they reached the jeep. He tilted the cup to get the last swallow of coarse-sugared milk, then threw the empty cup into the gutter. The children were still there, pitching five-piastre coins at cracks in the sidewalk, or spinning the coins against compound walls. They did not swarm around Knox and B.D. this time; they already knew them. But one boy with smallpox scars on his face looked at B.D. "Hey, GI, you numba ten." But none of his fellows looked up, so the child returned to his coin-throwing.

The streets were hot now and traffic was moving sluggishly. B.D. drove with his left foot outside the jeep. "You're going to get your leg broken doing that," Knox said.

B.D. ignored him. He drove with his standard great disregard for the rights of other traffic. Everyone else was doing the same thing, so he drove the way he did out of defense. He did not shift when he should have, and the engine lugged every time he cornered. Knox was tense and nervous because of the way B.D. drove. They turned onto Cong Ly at the corner of the palace grounds. Riot troops of the National Police Field Force wearing brown-dappled camouflage and small round wicker shields hung on their web belts stood on the sidewalk outside the tall iron fence. Concertina wire was looped in the gutter and movable chevaux-de-frise stood ready to slide into position to block the street. Few civilian vehicles were moving on Cong Ly.

Knox saw the bright parasols in the open park directly in front of the palace. The saffron robes of the bonzes sitting quietly beneath the parasols were surrounded by other men in riot gear and the white shirts of policemen. Their white and green jeeps were parked against the curbs and on the grass. A tarpulin had been stretched between the side of a half-ton truck and a tree to provide shade for a communications unit. "Looks like the Buddhists moved while we were in Cholon," Knox said.

"Yeah, Trich tri Quang probably moved from the An Quang Pagoda just about the time we left. There've been reports he's planning another confrontation about the elections. It wasn't supposed to be this soon, though."

"That must be Trich under the big umbrella, the one with all the white mice around it."

"Must be. He's the only bonze who can rate that much protection."

"We'd better get to the office. Those look like more demonstrators at the barricades farther down."

"Some more moving over there across from the cathedral. Oh shit, they look like students, and they're the worst kind."

But they did not reach the office immediately, or even get as far as John F. Kennedy Square. B.D. had turned into Han Thuyen because the lower end of Thong Nhut was blocked with police jeeps. A mob of young demonstrators was marching up Rue Pasteur behind some crudely lettered placards. They had almost reached the edge of the park before the police began to react. Police jeeps screamed past them and began blocking the intersection. Three big five-by trucks rumbled up from the opposite direction, where they had been parked out of sight behind the cathedral. Riot troops began throwing off coils of concertina wire. A half-ton truck with loudspeakers on the cab climbed the curbing and crossed the broad sidewalk to stop in front of the demonstrators. The demonstrators halted in front of the barricade, at least the front elements did. Other demonstrators were still coming from Pasteur. Some of them were filling the area out along the barricades, but others kept pushing in from the rear. The people in the center of the street were being pushed closer to the concertina wire. Three of the demonstrators in the forefront were trying to read a petition. The noise was getting louder and the riot police had pulled on gas masks. They were closing ranks and unsnapping their clubs.

B.D. was perspiring. He had the gears in neutral and was looking around for some place to go. The street was blocked ahead and more police reinforcements were arriving. They could not turn around, either. The sidewalk was filling up with riot troops on foot. "Oh Christ, we're in it now, we're fucked for sure." B.D. switched off the ignition.

The three demonstrators in the van had been joined by some Buddhist monks, but they had given up trying to read their petition and were attempting to hand it to a police lieutenant. He was standing in front of the riot troops with a microphone in his hand and calling for the demonstrators to disperse. His voice was being amplified through the sound truck behind him, but the angry hum of the crowd was rising above his words. The demonstrators in front kept trying to give their petition to the lieutenant and he kept shaking his head and telling them to disperse. One of the monks close to the lieutenant took the petition and rolled it into a tube. Then he threw it across the concertina wire at the police lieutenant. He ducked and a riot trooper pulled the pin on a tear gas grenade and threw it into the crowd.

More gas grenades were landing in the crowd and other riot police were coming up to reinforce those already at the barricades. One bonze blundered into the concertina wire and two policemen dragged him over the barbed wire while a third policeman beat at the monk with a club. The bonze had long gashes in his face and along his arms. Some paving stones were thrown and a policeman went down, but most of the riot police were pretty adept at warding off stones with their round wicker shields.

A phalanx of riot police behind shields and gas masks marched into the demonstrators. There was a lot of noise and some of the demonstrators were pulling on plastic bags as partial defense against the gas. The riot police went for them first. They were the seasoned ones, the ones who had been in riots before. Sirens warbled as more jeeps poured in. Two girls in Western dress darted out of a gas cloud and collided with a truck. They screamed as they fell down. Policemen had them on their feet instantly. One man ripped off one girl's dress and began slapping her breasts. Knox could hear the slaps even above the sirens and the shouting and the confusion.

B.D. suddenly started the engine. One of the police jeeps on their left had pulled forward and created an opening. "We're going. Hang on. I'll have to jump the curb."

They jumped the curb and drove on the grass for a hundred feet, then across the sidewalk and into the street again. A tendril of gas swirled around the jeep and B.D. hid his face in the crook of his arm and drove straight

ahead. They sideswiped a lamppost and the jeep step on
Knox's side crumpled. B.D. fought to maintain control.

Knox's eyes burned from the gas. He was coughing and
having trouble swallowing. "Watch where you're going,
you're about to hit the wire."

B.D. sawed at the wheel and drove parallel to the barricades for fifty yards. A sympathetic policeman pushed open
a cheval-de-frise for them and they shot through onto
Thong Nhut. B.D. did not stop until they were in the Embassy parking lot.

"The Chief is going to give us holy hell about that jeep
step," B.D. said.

"What about those poor bastards back there? They're
being dragged over barbed wire and getting their tits
slapped."

B.D. very carefully got out of the jeep and came around
to look at the twisted step. Dark perspiration stains extended down to his knees. "That's Vietnamese business.
It doesn't concern us. The Buddhists and the communists
put those people up to it. The Embassy told Thieu he should
hold down street demonstrations and not give them a chance
to get out of hand. You got to remember there's something
extra mean about an Asian. He's real amenable when you're
on your feet and looking him in the eye, but if you're down
he's naturally going to kick you in the nuts to make sure you
stay that way. If there had been more demonstrators the
police would have been the ones getting hell stomped out of
them." They were almost inside the Annex.

"Say, did you see that old Edsel parked out at the Cholon
PX today?"

"What about it?"

"Some of the Army troops from Long Bien wanted to buy
it. They're asking all the troops incountry to donate a

penny. They're going to buy that goddamn Edsel and ship it to McNamara. I bet he'll appreciate that."

"He doesn't strike me as a person who'd see much humor in that kind of present."

"Maybe he wouldn't, but four hundred thousand GIs would get a hell of a charge out of it."

Mister Balfour may have learned about the jeep's damaged step, but he did not say anything about it. He was good at finding out about the little things, the unimportant things. It was the big things, the important things, that he never could get to in time. He was closeted in his office all that afternoon with some high-ranking Vietnamese from the Directorate General of the National Police. The man with the long fingernails which curved from his little fingers like boars' tusks was one of them. They were still in Mister Balfour's office when Knox and B.D. stopped work early in the evening.

"Maybe nobody said anything about the step to him," Knox said hopefully.

"I'm sure somebody did, but unless they remind him he'll forget about it by tomorrow."

The demonstrators had long been forced from the park; the parasols were not visible in the early evening twilight, but the number of police jeeps parked around the main gate of the palace had not diminished. Some of the streets were still sealed off, but they had no difficulty getting through the barricades. They walked down the street the Vietnamese called Tu Do and which the French had called rue Catinat; like all other streets except Pasteur and Alex de Rhodes, it had been renamed after independence. Knox and B.D. walked because there were no taxis. No driver was rash enough to venture near the palace. It was not very far to walk anyway, and they were quickly downtown.

They settled on the My Canh floating restaurant as the place to eat. Tu Do was quiet. There was little noise and few Vietnamese civilians in the streets. Riot troops were on street corners and the barbed-wire barricades were stacked along the sidewalks. Side streets were not cordoned off, but all the same there was little traffic besides military vehicles. The lights in the bars still flashed their colorful names, but the music was subdued and there were few bargirls standing in the doorways. Two VNAF Skyraiders passed overhead, flying parallel to the street. They were just high enough to clear the top of the Caravelle.

Even the Saigon Departo was shuttered and locked. Only one beggar was on the street. B.D. bought a Saigon *Post* at the Indian bookstore next to Maxim's. He stuffed the cheap yellow paper into a hip pocket. They turned right at the Majestic and crossed Bach Dang to quayside. The docks were busy. Ships were berthed all along the quay and the involved process of discharging cargo was going on beneath the bright shipboard lights. Vehicular traffic was picking up.

They walked across the gangplank and up the side of the My Canh. The maître d' met them at the top and showed them to a corner table on the uncovered rear deck. A waiter brought beer and peanuts and took their order. B.D. spread the paper and began reading. He found an article which amused him. "Here's a piece about a girl who left her husband to live with an American Army sergeant. The husband killed himself this morning. The paper is all upset about it. Blaming us for loosening the morals of their women. Dumb bastard. He was chicken. He should have killed her and her lover." B.D. turned back to the paper and the comically misspelled words.

An American Export Ibrandsen freighter was docked a hundred yards away. Some children in a boat propelled by a small outboard motor with a long propeller shaft which made it easy to tilt the prop out of the water moved away from the counter of the vessel and headed for the My Canh. They had been scavenging for food in the garbage dumped overboard.

They held their position just astern of the My Canh in the sluggish tide and shouted up to the people on the open deck for food or piastres. B.D. ignored them but Knox threw them a small piastre coin. A young girl, tall for a Vietnamese, caught it and cried for more. Other diners threw bits of bread. One woman Knox recognized as a worker at JUSPAO threw them a can of cola. Her companion threw two coins. Another child caught one coin but the tall girl stretched on tiptoe and lost her balance. She fell half-overboard but caught the gunwale as she hit the water. The boy at the helm helped her into the boat. The girl's white pantaloons were greasy with slime and oil. But she had the coin in her teeth.

A light rain began to fall. The waiters stopped serving long enough to crank out the metal awning. Since they were sitting in the corner some faint mist blew in from time to time, but it was not enough to make them move. "Don't blame me if those kids put a limpet charge on the hull and blow us out of the water," B.D. said.

"I'm not worried. You told me this place paid VC taxes after they were hit by the claymores."

"Anybody who just fell into the Saigon River should be mad enough to do anything."

"They're Vietnamese."

"It's not like feeding animals at a zoo."

"You don't sound like the same B.D. who met me at the airport. You were saying something about test-tube birth."

"I can blow hot or I can blow cold."

"You were blowing hot today."

"There's a difference between dissent and disagreement. Those people today were stupid. Or they were naive, which is just as bad. You can do all sorts of things when you're naive and think you're right, but those people were trying to pull down something which isn't built yet and they don't have anything to put up in its place. That's the hell of it."

"Maybe they had some real grievances. That police lieutenant never looked at their petition."

"I don't doubt that in the least, but when you're fighting for your survival you don't have time to argue about how it's done. I don't like some of the things Ky has done any better than some of the things Minh did, or Diem, or the rest, but —" B.D. broke off. The waiter was bringing their food and more beer.

"But what?"

"Nothing. You haven't been out here long enough. It's no good talking about it. Not to you."

"You make it sound like a religion of your own. I've been here over four months now. I'm no virgin."

"Maybe it is my own brand of religion. You can't be around people without their getting to you in some way. The Viets are no different. No matter what I might say, I like them. I hate them, too. They've labored long for the privilege of being indifferent. When we get them on their feet they'll kick us out, but at least they'll be standing on their own goddamn feet when they do it."

"You don't sound like the same old B.D."

"Like I said. I can blow hot or I can blow cold. I got to believe what I believe otherwise I've wasted a perfectly good portion of my life. Take you and Rosette. You can't go around seeing a person like you've been seeing Rosette without getting some emotions tangled up."

"I've been through a divorce. I think I know how to stay

ahead of my emotions without letting myself get tangled up."

"You stupid fucking fool. I'm not talking about your god-damn feelings. I'm talking about her. She's got feelings too."

"That's all right," Knox said. But he wondered if it was. For that matter if he was. "It's not your problem."

"Problems are mostly matters of nomenclature. People get upset at the thought that a particular name may or may not apply to them. But you got to understand it's you, not somebody else, who puts that name on yourself in the first place. So if you know that, you can see that you also can take the name off and the problem's half-solved."

"You don't make sense."

"I never make sense. You haven't noticed before?" B.D. finished the last of his beer. The woman from JUSPAO had drunk the last of a cola. She threw the can into the river. Both she and the man with her laughed as it bobbled in the wake of a passing junk. B.D. looked at her for a moment without blinking. "Goddamn woman."

"A subject when fairly once begun should not be left till all that should be said is done. Shakespeare said that."

"He did, did he? Well possum shit. B.D. Drummond said that. You got a few words wrong, but that doesn't matter. I can't remember them either." B.D. belched heavily. The woman at the next table stared at him. B.D. waved at her. "Hello, dearie. Haven't I seen you at the five-o'clock fol-lies?" The woman turned back to her companion.

"We'd better get out of here. The rain's stopped."

They settled the bill and walked down the gangplank. "You see much of Davies?"

"Calvin?" Knox was immediately on the defensive. "Oh, he comes around sometimes when he's in town. Has a drink. Never stays long."

"Stay away from him. He's in the market in a big way and one of these days he's going to get up tight with the police and busted big. A lot of people with him are going to get busted, too. Whether they're in the market or not won't matter. He'll say they are. Just wanted to give you a little friendly advice about him."

"Who'd believe a liar?"

"A lot of people. You'd be surprised."

They reached the end of the gangplank and touched pavement. Traffic was almost normal now. There were a lot of cyclos and taxis moving. The sultry heat had dried most of the rain, but a few patches of asphalt steamed and a few puddles stood in depressions. The night air close to the street was once again its normal pale exhaust blue. B.D. held up a hand and whistled. A taxi driver saw them and began making a U-turn against the traffic. They were both watching the taxi and did not see the cyclo until it was too late. It came out of the glare of a car's headlights, materializing suddenly. Its metal basket was real enough, though.

"Watch out," Knox said, and stepped back. He heard a sound like the snapping of a twig wrapped in a wet towel. B.D. went down on his back in the steam and the damp and Knox stared around in bewilderment. There were several cyclos going away from him. They all looked alike.

He looked down at B.D. B.D. was trying to raise himself on bruised elbows. His face was unnaturally white and large splotches of sweat had broken out all over it. His right leg was straight except for the ankle. It was twisted at an oblique angle to the calf. B.D. rolled over on his stomach and beat the pavement with his fist. "It hurts, goddamn, it hurts."

Knox was kneeling beside him. Some children were clustering around. He chased them away. Knox wondered briefly where they came from. He had seen no children within fifty yards when they walked off the My Canh.

"Get help. Try that for a start," snapped B.D.

"Want me to straighten your foot?"

"Goddamn NO."

Knox tried to flag down a flat-bed truck carrying cargo from the docks, but it drove past him. He tried several others without success. Then he saw a Korean Army jeep with a long radio antenna bent down over the top. The jeep was half a block away and going toward the port, but he shouted and ran after it. The passenger saw him and punched the driver in the ribs. The jeep stopped and Knox caught up with it. He was out of breath, but he managed to tell the Koreans what had happened and what he needed.

One of the Koreans understood English fairly well. He got on the radio and tried to raise someone at the Third Field Hospital. All he got was static. "I can't get Americans," he said. "Too much structures in the way."

"Nothing works when you want it to."

"I suppose this possible we carry your friend. Can he sit?"

They drove back to where B.D. lay. He was fending off the children from the wharf. Knox saw the woman from JUSPAO and her companion getting into a taxi up the street. B.D. was whispering something into closed fists. Knox bent down.

"The bitch. She walked right past me and didn't stop. Laughed and said something about what happened to drunks served them right. That cunt, that stupid fucking cunt."

"Can you sit in a jeep? I've got some Koreans who'll take us to the Third Field if you can sit."

"You bet your ass I can sit. I'm fine. Some kid made off with my watch and a cunt just walked by and laughed at me. But I'm fine. Just get me to a hospital. I'm fine."

Hue

I

B.D. WAS IN A HOSPITAL WARD with his foot in traction, and Knox was making the courier run to Hue B.D. had originally been scheduled to make. He stopped by the Third Field on his way to Tan son Nhut and left B.D. some cigarettes, but B.D. was asleep so Knox put the cigarettes under his pillow so no one would steal them and went on to the airport. He was flying up to Hue in an Air Force C-47 psyops plane because Air America had been unable to get him to Hue before midnight. He sat part of the time on a bale of propaganda leaflets and kept the briefcase of documents close to him. The plane was going to drop leaflets over a hamlet area on the coast between Nha Trang and Tuy Hoa. The area was not contested and the drop would be routine; otherwise he could not have gotten on the flight with his satchel of documents that someone at CAS Headquarters had designated as sensitive information.

Knox pulled some leaflets out of a bale and studied them. He recognized some Chieu Hoi passes and a lot of other pamphlets he had seen at the mission. One paper showed two children and a woman hanging from the shattered windows of an overturned bus. The picture was brutal and he had no doubt the smudged captions were equally hard sell.

"Who makes up this trash?" he asked the load master, who was sitting across from him masticating a wad of Beechnut chewing tobacco.

"They're printed in Saigon, some of them, but a lot are printed in Manila and brought in."

"I don't mean that. Who writes this garbage?"

"They got teams of funky people at Seventh Air Force who do nothing but think up things to say." The load master paused to spit into an empty Dixie cup he kept handy. "Westmoreland sometimes dashes off a slogan or two and the psyops people grind it out. It's bad stuff though; you wouldn't turn yourself in if you were a Charlie. Might keep a few in your pocket for potty paper, but it hasn't made anybody rally that I've heard about." The load master's jaws moved and he spat into the cup from time to time.

Knox peered out a window at the coastline below. The weather was good, not like the last time he had flown. The sea was so calm he could not see whitecaps. They flew over a city with a pleasant curving bay and an island offshore. He asked the load master where they were and the load master said they were over Nha Trang and the island was Hon Tri. Knox could feel the plane descending gradually. The load master put on a pair of earphones connected to a long trail of signal wire and went back to the hoppers set up by the cargo door. Another crewman joined him and began slitting open the bales of propaganda leaflets. The C-47 dropped lower and lower and the two crewmen crouched by the hoppers. The crew chief looked up and gave Knox the okay sign with thumb and forefinger. "No sweat," he said. But Knox did not hear him over the noise of the engines. The pilot gave them the word and the two men began dumping leaflets into the hoppers. As soon as they had gone through one bale and started on another the load master dragged two more bales to the hopper and broke them open.

Knox remained at his window. The plane was maybe one thousand feet above the forest. They were flying in a shallow circle and he could see leaflets fluttering down as they continued to bank. But he saw no hamlets, not even isolated rice fields or solitary houses.

The crewmen stopped dumping leaflets before they had dropped half the bales and the load master went forward to the cockpit. He came back in a few minutes and pinched some more tobacco into his cheek.

"Are you through with the drop?"

"Hell, no. We dropped in the wrong place. Somebody gave us the wrong coordinates. Or the copilot can't navigate worth a shit. We missed the real drop zone by thirty miles. The captain says he's not going back, and we're just going to shove the rest of the bales. The captain, he don't want to deviate from the flight plan. The flight plan calls for one sustained drop in so many minutes, and he's not turning around. We're going to swing out over the water above Qui Nhon City to miss all the troop aircraft moving through there. We'll drop what we got left and go on to Hue."

The load master started to drag bales closer to the cargo door, but the copilot called back to say they were changing the center of gravity. The crew chief stopped shifting the bales, but after a while they opened the door all the way and pushed the first bale of leaflets through the door. The load master lay on his back and supported himself with his elbows while the other crewman moved the bales into position in front of the door, then the load master gave each bale a slight push with his feet and the bale tumbled out.

They dropped all the leaflets between Qui Nhon and Da Nang. There were a lot of leaflets but they were all dropped in a long string of splashes into the blue waters of the South China Sea where the saltwater quickly soaked into the cheap, porous paper, and after a time the bales sank before they ever had a chance to drift ashore in Binh Dinh Province.

II

When the C-47 touched down at Phu Bai airport Knox was little more than one hundred kilometers south of the Seventeenth Parallel. The supply base as Phu Bai was like any other forward supply point: dusty, raw; building materials, equipment, storage containers piled haphazardly wherever had been most convenient for the fork-lift operator at the time he got tired of carrying it.

He knew no one from CAS would be at the airport to meet him, so he hitched a ride to Hue with a USAID official who was driving a battered gray pickup which had the right half of the windshield broken out. The pickup body was loaded with bulgar wheat in hundred-pound sacks, and the truck springs did little to cushion the ride. Knox was wearing his Air Force sunglasses, but even they did not keep his eyes from smarting in the blast of air through the shattered windshield. The USAID man, who had introduced himself as Hjort, suddenly turned off the main highway and began driving down a dirt road which was little more than a cattle path.

"What gives?" Knox said. "I've got to get to Hue."

"I'll get you there," Hjort said. "Making a little detour first. Got wheat to deliver."

"Away from Hue?"

"Got to go the way the road goes."

Knox put his bag of documents beneath the seat and anchored them with his shoes. He touched his elbow to the window ledge but jerked it away because the metal was blistering hot. The road was heavily rutted and Hjort drove slowly. They passed a few houses and huts but they appeared deserted. The road descended into a small valley with a lot of small tombs before it started to climb again. The road led through two large tombs situated in a curve. A Vietnamese in faded *au babas* with sandals cut from old automobile tires stood in the middle of the road. He was aiming an AK-47 at them. Hjort very prudently stopped. It was exactly one o'clock by Knox's watch. Two more men got up from the tall grass at the edge of the road, and a forth guerrilla appeared on top of the nearest tomb. The guerrilla in the road slung his carbine over his shoulder and walked toward them. Hjort relaxed down into the seat and switched off the engine. "No sweat," he said. "They're just local VC collecting some tax."

"What are they after, the wheat?"

"Not when they see it's bulgar." Hjort lapsed into silence because the Viet Cong had reached them and was tentatively poking the contents of the bulgar sacks with a dirty forefinger. He made a grimace of disgust.

"Bo-le-ga," he called to his companions. One of the men in the tall grass trotted up to join him but the other two kept their rifles trained casually on the truck cab. Knox had the same feeling of unease he had had when the white mice had stopped the Lambretta minibus in Saigon. The two Viet Cong pulled a sack from the bottom of the load and slit it open with a carbine bayonet. They hefted the sack and poured the contents over the tailgate. Hjort drummed his fingers soundlessly on the rim of the steering wheel. It was bulgar all right. The second Viet Cong came around to Hjort's side and put out his hand. "Dong," he said. "Mon-ei."

Hjort took out his wallet and handed the Viet Cong all

the money he had. The Viet Cong carefully counted it and showed it to the other guerrilla. The other man took the money, recounted it, then returned half the bills to Hjort. He leaned over the hood of the truck and wrote out a receipt with a ball-point pen. He gave the receipt to Hjort. Then he motioned to Knox. "Same-same," he said. "Quick-quick." Knox took out his wallet and handed it to the Viet. He had to lean across Hjort and his briefcase slid out from under the seat. The Viet counted Knox's currency and returned exactly half of it. He pointed at the briefcase. Knox ignored the Viet. The Viet motioned again, this time a little sharper.

"He wants the bag," Hjort said.

"I can't give it to him."

"Give him the bag before he kills you and looks for himself."

Knox slowly handed the briefcase across Hjort. "It's locked," he said. The Vietnamese put the bag on the hood of the truck and tugged at one lock. It came open. He tried the other lock. It refused to open so he ran a bayonet between the metal tongue and the lock. The tongue flicked open. The Viet ran a hand through the papers. Then he dumped the briefcase in the truck bed. Some of the papers with the large black SECRET stamp across the top and bottom of the colored-paper cover sheets spilled out of the briefcase and fell down between the grain sacks. Knox watched the papers through the dusty rear window. The Viet motioned for them to go. He had not given Knox a receipt for his money.

Hjort started the engine and let out the clutch. They jolted away from the tombs. "Stop as soon as you get a chance," Knox said. "Those are classified papers."

"I'm not stopping until we're out of sight. The VC would come over to check us out."

143

"We could outrun them."

"Not in this truck we couldn't, and they could cut over the ridges to get ahead of us for sure."

Knox kept looking back through the rear window until a turning of the road finally hid the Viet Cong from view. "Stop now. They can't see us anymore."

"Don't take long," Hjort said. Knox got out of the cab and clambered over the side of the bed. He found the brief-case and began stuffing papers into it. He gathered all the documents he could find and got back inside the cab.

"Got them all?"

"I don't know. I haven't got a list of what's supposed to be here."

Hjort glanced at the documents Knox was trying to stuff into the briefcase and whistled. "You've got some hot stuff there. How come you're riding with me?"

"Because you offered me a ride and I thought you were going straight to Hue."

"Hell, you should have waited. I didn't know you had anything like that. You're lucky the VC couldn't read English."

"They're probably not important. But the thing is I'm signed for them. It'll be my ass if anything happens to them." Knox got all the papers back in the briefcase and closed it. He tugged at the locks. They sprang open. "How come they didn't kill us? Why'd they take only half our money?"

Hjort sighed. "The government isn't very strong in this area. Neither are the Charlies. Right now. Nobody wants to make waves, you know what I mean. As far as I know, there aren't many North Vietnamese regulars operating around here. The Charlies are mostly local types so it's a family thing where some are with the government and some are with the VC. The VC use this region as a rest area.

They figure it's okay to stop people and rob them. Tax. If they killed anybody, though, the government might move in some troops and nobody'd like that. At least that's how I figure it."

Knox kept snapping and opening the locks. They rode in silence for another five kilometers. They entered a small hamlet of five or six houses. Children clad only in shirts which stopped at their waists played in the bare earthen yards where a few chickens pecked hopefully. An old man and woman peered hesitantly from the doorway of one house. They evidently recognized Hjort because the old man came down the sagging steps of the crude ladder and stood talking to them. Hjort replied in broken Vietnamese. The old man clapped his hands and three girls just entering puberty trooped demurely out of the house. They padded across the yard and began unloading the sacks of bulgar. It took all three to lift one sack. Knox stood by the cab to see if the girls would uncover any documents he had missed. He found none.

The girls carried and half dragged the sacks into the house until the truck was empty. The old man gestured for Hjort and Knox to go inside. He sat them at a bare wooden table on hard wooden chairs and they drank very weak tea from small cups in filagree baskets without handles. "Why did you give all that wheat to this old man?"

"Because he uses it. He's the headman of this hamlet and he uses bulgar like nobody uses bulgar." Hjort pointed to a large caldron bubbling on top of the small clay stove. The old woman was feeding straw into the fire. "He feeds it to the hamlet's pigs."

Knox's surprise must have showed. Hjort shrugged. "No Vietnamese will eat it. These riceburners can't get used to it. It's like asking them to eat birdseed. They've always eaten rice. They don't want to eat anything but rice. They believe they can't eat anything but rice. But we send out thousands of tons of bulgar wheat and tell the Vietnamese it's good for them. They'd rather starve first." Hjort paused as the old man poured them another bit of tea. "Most people we give it to throw it out. Some mix it with cement in place of sand. One or two Vietnamese ferment it and make moonshine. This old man at least puts it to good use. It feeds the hogs, the hogs feed him."

"If the VC don't get the hogs first."

"Yes, that could happen, but the old man pays tax, too. He gets hit by Saigon, the province, some absentee landlord probably, and the VC. He gets a royal screwing. But he makes do. That's all he's worried about. All he wants to do is farm his little piece of land and worship his ancestors. He doesn't give a flying fuck how this country is run or who runs it."

"Why is the old woman cooking the wheat?"

"The hogs won't eat it unless it's cooked." They finished their tea and Hjort made his good-byes to the old man.

"You aren't going back the way you came, are you?"

"No, there's another way. It's longer but it goes through a populated area and the VC won't show themselves around there in the daytime."

They drove for half an hour on the primitive road before they came to a fork and turned right. A few kilometers further they passed a large stone courtyard with several small slender stone towers around it and tiered steps leading up to it. Knox thought it was an old palace but Hjort said it was Khai Dinh's Tomb. They sped through a village of more than average size. The road was paved now. Ten kilometers later they entered the outskirts of Hue, crossed Huong Giang, the River of Perfumes, close to the point where the Truong Sisters had drowned themselves when the Chinese reinvaded Vietnam and they could not rally their people to drive out the Chinese as they had done once before. Knox got out of the truck in front of the Noontime Gate. Hjort gave him a cheerful wave and said they would probably meet again. Knox said he hoped so, without really meaning it, and walked off to find the CAS office.

He turned in his briefcase and told the administrative clerk in the outer office that the locks did not work. The clerk asked him how he knew the locks were insecure and Knox said he had fallen in the plane and the locks had opened. The clerk left the room and came back a minute later with a typed list. He compared all the documents Knox had brought with the items on the list. At length he said he was satisfied everything was there, but how did some of the papers get flour on them? Knox said he did not know, he was just a courier and he did not like having to look after a damned briefcase anyway and he hoped he would never be a courier again. The clerk said Knox was out of luck on that point because the agent in charge had a priority Phoenix report for Knox to carry back to Saigon. The clerk told Knox he had a room for the night at the Hue Hotel on Le Loi, and if Knox would wait for half an hour or so an agent who lived in the hotel would drive him over.

Knox sat in the hot office in a dusty government issue swivel chair beneath a ceiling fan and leafed through a tattered months-old issue of *Time*. He did not find anything to interest him and put it aside to sit in the stir of air with dust rising in a thin nebula around him. People began to leave the offices in the back. Two Vietnamese went out the street entrance and a little later the working agents came out. A bearded American with a high forehead and a dead pipe in his teeth walked over and offered his hand. "Knox from Headquarters, I presume."

"The same."

"I'm Chenowith. I've got a chap over at the hotel who

sez he knows you. One of the agents up from Phan Rang on a little business to Cambodia for us."

Chenowith had a Mini-Moke. It was parked in the back within a small courtyard with an iron gate and a Nung guard in a sandbagged kiosk beside it. They moved through the gate and into the traffic. Dusk was not far off but there was a tranquility about the city which Knox had never known in Saigon. The evening air was very still, and he heard the mellow strike of the Great Big Bell in the Linh Mu Pagoda. The Mountain of the King was visible as a vague pink bulge in the distance, though ethereal in the failing light and last haze of afternoon heat. They crossed the river via the Gia Vien Bridge and turned onto Le Loi. They drove past a group of Dong Khanh schoolgirls with book satchels under their arms. Their long hair hung down past their waists, and even though they were young they already moved and were marked with the innocent sensuousness of their race and their sex. Knox turned to watch them as the Mini-Moke slid past. They were like all women, girls or old spinsters: undefeated, undefeatable, unsurrendered and indomitable, unreconciled and irreconcilable, unvanquished, unannealed, timeless, though out of another age, another milieu. Prologue and epitaph, woman's epitome, ageless, enduring. Woman.

Fumarole was sitting on the verandah of the hotel when they parked the Mini-Moke and walked up the low steps. He did not get up to greet them but waved toward chairs. "How are things at the piranha bowl?" he asked Knox.

"Same-same. Some Buddhist demonstrations, some students, too. But no monk's cremated himself yet. B.D. was hit by a cyclo and broke his ankle. He was to have made this trip."

"I heartily recommend their gin and tonic. Like everything else in this goddamn place it's outrageously overpriced. Was it an accident or a deliberate attempt to get him?"

"Hard to say. I was with him. We were watching something else and didn't see the cyclo until it was on top of us. Mister Balfour tends to think it was an accident."

"You can't be sure of something like that unless you get the cyclo driver and make him talk." Fumarole shook his head. "You can't be sure of anything in this business."

He raised his glass. "Here's to B.D.'s health. At least he didn't break his third leg."

A Vietnamese in Western dress which included a necktie and German-made rose-tinted glasses appeared at the edge of the verandah and looked around hesitantly. Chenowith brought him over and the Viet sat down at the table with them. He was ill at ease, almost as if he were a guest in his own country. "This is Bui," Chenowith said. "He's a graduate medical student who's working with some French priests on the coast. I invited him over to dinner tonight."

"Where did you study medicine?" Fumarole asked.

"In Paris. Presently we have a new hospital and I have the much work to do there."

"What kind of hospital?"

"A sanatorium for sufferers of the leprosy." Bui turned to Knox. "You have just come from Saigon?"

"Yes, this afternoon."

"So you must know when the war will end."

"No, I do not know when the war will end."

"Oh yes you do," Bui said in a very matter-of-fact voice. He blinked his eyes rapidly behind his German glasses. "All Americans in Saigon know, but you can't tell us."

There was an awkward pause. Then Fumarole said, "We all hope the war will end soon."

"Yes, it is certain. We do not like to see people die. It reminds us of our own mortality."

"You speak English very well."

"Yes, thank you. I studied in your school at Notre Dame thank you to the Maryknoll Fathers."

"A fine school."

"Of certainty. I wanted to stay in your country because I was safe there. I know I do not have much time left. Very soon the VC will come. Even to Hue. Because I am a doctor they will kill me."

"You seem very certain of that," Chenowith said.

"Oh yes, very certain. One is never mistaken in these matters."

"They are very important matters."

"Of certainty. But my ancestors are here. One must die where one is welcomed."

"It is never good to die in a strange place."

"Yes, that is why I sorrow for your young men who die here. Your country must have much young men that you can afford to lose so many."

"We have many young men," Fumarole said, "but we can't afford to lose any of them"

"Have you finished your hospital yet?" This from Chenowith.

"The fathers finished the building last week and we opened it the day late. We had every bed filled by the afternoon. Oh, so quickly did they come. And we were all so proud of the hospital. We even had flushing toilets thanks to your U-S-A-I-D programs. I myself put the toilet paper rolls in the stalls. I was very proud that my people would have such a thing. But later the fathers came to me and say that the toilets were stoppered. We had show the people how to use the toilets, but they had take the paper from the stalls to make cigarettes." Bui spread his hands helplessly. "Such paper for making cigarettes they had never seen. The wards were filled with much smoke. If you had seen.

They saved the papers from the toilets and used the old newspapers. We have much backwards in my people. I will be sorry not to be here."

No one answered him. Bui seemed very certain of himself. The swift tropic night had softly enwrapped them. Some colored-paper lanterns floated quietly in the slow rippleless current of the river. Pulled along by something older than the water and the earth and the dreams of the people who launched them. They sat quietly for a time and watched the candles flickering through the thin tissue of the lanterns.

A group of ARVN soldiers came into view along the street. They wore the dim illumination from the streetlamps like outer garments. They were walking slowly along the riverbank, walking slowly and watching the paper lanterns. An American jeep with at least six GIs in it raced up Le Loi. They drew even with the ARVN soldiers. "ARVN mother-fuckin' sonsofbitches," one of the soldiers shouted. The driver of the jeep blew his horn derisively. Everyone on the verandah heard the GI.

Bui got to his feet and bowed slightly. His nostrils were pinched. "I must go back to hospital. I have take much of your time already." Chenowith started to say something, then stopped because Bui bowed again and walked away quickly. He went down the steps and turned in the direction the group of ARVN soldiers had taken. They were left alone on the verandah with the cicadas and the floating too soon extinguished and destroyed paper lanterns.

"He seems to be a very ardent young man," Fumarole said.

"He is. Damn those GIs. They had no business calling those ARVNs sonsofbitches."

"I rode up from Phu Bai yesterday," Fumarole said. "I hitched a ride in a Marine ton-and-a-half. One of the Marines kept aiming his M-sixteen at every Viet we passed. He kept saying he didn't trust any goddamn gook, even the Koreans."

"That's going from antipathy, which is a physical fact, to hate, which is a state of mind."

"Who's to blame for that?"

"Hell, blame anybody you want. Everybody's guilty. I don't have the answer. If I did I'd bottle it and sell it to the politicians. Chenowith's patent elixir for relieving guilt, lifting depression, restoring confidence. Good for everything, from giving purpose to this war to curing warts."

"Roger that. The palliative of national purpose. In sixty-six Uncle Ho promised to fight for five, ten, twenty years. Then Johnson tells the troops to bring back that coonskin for the wall. Who're you going to believe?"

"That's too much for me. I just wonder if Bui knows something we should know."

"What more can we do? We make out an IIR every time a VC takes a crap and send it down to Saigon in triplicate. We tell them how it looked, how much it weighed, even describe the smell. Saigon sees no big push. They're supposed to collate these reports from all over the republic. They've got the Big Picture. Your friend's just depressed because his patients used his nice clean tee paper for fags and wiped their asses with newsprint."

III

Knox awoke before dawn. The room was smaller than his bedroom in Saigon and this room had two double beds in it. He was perspiring heavily and felt dirty all over his body. There was a gecko stirring somewhere in the room. Knox could hear the tremulous scurry of his suction-cup feet across the ceiling. He lay there in the coolness and breathed shallowly and regularly and wondered why he was perspiring. Gradually he stopped perspiring. He wanted to go back to sleep, but was afraid, and some inner clock told him it was already too late. So he lay in the stillness which he shared with Fumarole and the gecko and thought of Rosette until the grayish tinge of first light began to soften through the window. After a while there was enough light to see fairly well and he knew that Fumarole was awake because the sheets on his bed hissed as he rolled. Then Fumarole got out of bed.

Knox continued to breathe slowly. Fumarole crossed in front of the window with his kit bag under his arm. His legs were unbelievably long and hairy below his shorts. Fumarole soundlessly opened the louvered glass door to the small balcony outside their room which overlooked the River of Perfumes and the decayed Peking-style elegance of the old walled city. It was light enough now for Knox to see the King's Knight Flag Tower rising above the Citadel.

Fumarole sat on a wicker stool and began taking things out of the kit bag. He opened a small can of C-ration peanut butter with a GI can opener and sprayed it with GI insect repellent. Then he struck a match and touched it to the can. It burned like sterno. Fumarole twisted a piece of coat hanger wire around a can of beans and franks and held it over the small flame. When they were hot enough he spooned out the beans and franks with hard crackers. He drank from a gin bottle he held between his knees.

Knox sat up in bed. "What the hell are you doing?"

Fumarole started and broke a cracker. Beans fell on his bare knees. He scraped them off with a forefinger and flicked them over the balcony. "I expected you to sleep another thirty minutes or so."

Knox walked over to the glass door. The floor was cool

and felt good against his bare feet. It reminded him of child-
hood and walks along a deserted beach with his toes relishing every step in the damp sand. But that was all a long
time ago, and perhaps it had never really happened.

"I was awake before you came out and started eating
breakfast."

"I am eating breakfast," Fumarole said. The sun was full
up now and Knox noticed the thick tracery of wrinkles on
Fumarole's neck. The stubble of his beard was almost en-
tirely white.

"I've got two daughters in college back in the States. It
was my great misfortune to have daughters. Do you have
any idea what it costs to raise girls, particularly in modern-
day America? I hope they elope if they get married. I can't
afford to marry them off and educate them, too."

"I'm sorry, I won't tell anyone."

"About my daughters, everybody knows that."

"No, I meant — "

"I know what you meant and I'd appreciate it if you
wouldn't. You stay in this business long enough and you get
a reputation. And after a while you realize you uncon-
sciously encouraged it all along." Fumarole drank from
the gin bottle. "We're good imitations, both of us. No, not
the real thing, but good imitations. That's just as well since
the real things can step out of character and relax, but we
got to spend our time pretending to be one step above the
real thing."

"We're more real than reality itself," Knox said. "Then
we get tripped up by a little thing like peanut butter." He
went back inside and dressed. He put on the same clothes
he had worn the day before. He had not brought a suitcase.
He was learning. But he did not have any toilet articles either and wanted to brush his teeth very badly. Fumarole
continued to eat the beans and franks even though they had

grown quite cold. He did not look up when Knox left the room.

Knox picked up another briefcase of papers and the Phoenix report at the CAS office. He signed for the briefcase and Chenowith drove him to a helicopter pad near the stadium. He caught an Army helicopter all the way to Da Nang and rode a C-130 from Da Nang to Saigon. There were a lot of planes heading south that day and he had no trouble getting a ride in one of the fifteen seats normally blocked off for newspapermen on almost every incountry C-130 flight. Two weeks later when B.D. got out of the Third Field he told Knox that Fumarole was dead. He had gotten roaring drunk on *nuoc nep,* the potent rice wine, while in Cambodia and a nervous Cambodian policeman shot him when he refused to stop while driving the wrong way down a one-way street.

The Area under the Curve

TRUE HAD STAYED in the villa while Knox was in Hue. He had stayed only the one night and part of the day, and Knox had not seen him. He was back at the end of the month, though, and he was worried. He called Knox from the military side of Tan son Nhut when he flew in, and Knox told him the key was still in the urn by the steps and for him to make himself at home until Knox got off work. True said all right, but please get off as soon as possible because True had a problem. A big problem. And maybe Knox had a problem, too.

Knox took the most direct route to his villa, past faded walls covered with political posters just beginning to peel, along streets where women in *nha que* hats tied under their chins with dingy scarves were shoveling mud and debris from the gutters. By the bicycle repair stalls set up under spread ponchos at every street corner, where young boys constantly dirtied by the smoke and grease of their trade mended inner tubes in the afternoon, to his villa, where True waited.

"Mai's going to have a baby," True said. "I need to borrow fifty thousand piastres."

Knox sat down in one of the plastic-covered armchairs. True had a bottle of rum and an open Coke on the coffee table. Knox took the Coke and drank it from the can. He was very thirsty from the fast walk. "Why do you need that much?"

"To give to Mai so she can go away to have the baby."

"You don't even know if it's yours."

"Hell's bells, she told me. Shit, man, she's in love with me. The goddamn stupid broad's in love with me, playing it straight arrow."

"How long you known her? Two months?" Knox had finished the Coke so he put down the empty can. "That time enough for a baby to begin to show?"

"Christ man, can you imagine what'll happen if word gets back to my boss? He'd finish me. Remember that bit in the paper just after I first met you, about the Air Force doctor who knocked up a Vietnamese broad? Well, the guy did. She was a whore pure and simple and she was out for a rich American. He was a doctor so he offered to abort her, but she wanted the money. Planted articles in all the papers and the brass at Seventh Air Force really got up tight. Momeyer, that cocksucker, wanted to court-martial, disgrace the guy." True paused for breath and another drink.

"What happened to him? I'm not familiar with the story."

"Who?"

"Your doctor friend."

"He transferred. He was getting out, you know the Air Force can't keep doctors, and they couldn't hold him."

"If it didn't hurt him it won't hurt you."

"Yeah, but I'm not at the end of my tour. I could get really screwed up, conduct unbecoming an officer and gentleman or something like that. I tell you, those bastards at Seventh are really looking for someone to hang. They'd shove it up my ass and break it off."

157

"Give her the money and you'll never see her or the money again."

"Are you going to loan me the money?"

"No."

True breathed very hard. "Is it because you don't have that much money?"

"I've got the money. I just think Mai's playing you for a sucker."

True squeezed the Coke can in the middle until the metal buckled and the ends met. "Then I'm going to hunt up that big fat friend of yours and let him know you've been changing money. You and Calvin Davies. He turned me down, too."

Knox got up and went to the kitchen. He removed the small kick plate from the bottom of the refrigerator, and brought out the metal cake box. The box had contained a fruitcake his mother sent for Christmas. She always sent things early. His mother was very methodical. That was one reason he did not like his mother. He had given the cake to B.D. while he was in the hospital and never acknowledged his mother's letter. Knox had to pry at the lid because the lid was tight and closely fitted. But he got it off and took out a sheaf of thousand-piastre notes. He counted out fifty of them onto the dusty floor and put the box and the kick plate back as they were.

The electricity went off. The air conditioner stopped and the stream of bubbles from the aquarium pump gurgled once or twice before the bubbles stopped, too. The heat started in with a vengeance. Knox threw the piastres into True's lap. True tried to smile, but Knox motioned him out. True left. They knew too much about each other for him not to. Knox sat in the prickly heat of late afternoon with a vast numbness inside him where previously only an empty void had been. But sure enough, after a while that feeling passed, too, just as he knew it would.

II

Knox was sleeping late again. Because it was another Sunday and the days, the weeks, had fled into each other as they had a habit of doing. B.D. was gone a lot and Mister Balfour took little notice of Knox, so he did as he pleased, mostly. Nothing really stood out, nothing exceptional happened that he noted, or wanted to notice, so time slipped by and that was not exceptional either.

Rosette had not come to the house the night before; perhaps she would say she had visited friends. Perhaps she would say the Chinese did not have enough MPC for the green she took to Cholon yesterday; and she had had to wait, or return later. He did not care. She would come. He knew that.

He heard her heels click on the tile porch, then there was no sound for a few moments as she fumbled in the big flowerpot for the key. Then the key scraped in the lock and the bolt was thrown twice. Rosette came in softly. She put the key back in the flowerpot and closed the door. The bright, brittle heel clicks followed her across the floor. Then the rustle of a parcel being put down gently. Silence again, then the silibant bubbling of water as she poured new fish and then mosquito larvae into the aquarium.

Knox was lying on his belly with his head pillowed on his arm when she came into the room. She had taken off her shoes before she left the aquarium, and she entered the bedroom with hardly a sound. She sat down gently on the side of the bed so as not to disturb him and drew nebulous cir-

159

cles on his back, ever so softly. He feigned sleep and did not move. She tired of that and bent to kiss his neck. Her hair was down and the tips brushed across his shoulders. Knox shivered involuntarily and opened one eye.

"You awake all time," she said.

"No, I'm just waking up. Where's you been?"

"Cholon. Moneychanger away by police. Take all his money."

"You weren't scared, were you?"

"No. I no 'fraid change money. His wife know other money. I wait. Change all money I have. I 'fraid of other things."

"What things?" She was massaging his back now and he gave himself up to the pure animal luxury of it. He was really only half-listening to her.

"The VC. Many peoples know you are the main one in American plain intelligent."

"What do you mean, 'plain intelligent'?"

"No wear uniform. Very important that way. More than wear uniform. Other girls treat me with nice that no have if I bargirl live with American."

"Who busted the Chinaman? National Police or the military?"

"Both. Americans too. Work together. Men in uniforms, Army polices, men from National Police of General Loan. He wicked."

"Who? Loan?"

"Yes, peoples much afraid of him."

"He's not that bad. Just a cop doing his job. I've met him a couple of times."

"He friend of Ky. Ky go Loan go. If Loan go Ky go."

"Ky's not going to go. And Loan's dug in pretty deep."

Rosette was still massaging his back and he was almost asleep again.

"All same, Loan no friend Vietnamese. He no keep VC out. Plenty VC in Saigon. They look for me."

"You've been doing a good job of turning them in. There can't be many left."

"You make joke. Plenty VC. It no good for me to turn them to National Police. VC kill informers."

"You use other people to finger the VC. They can't put anything to you."

"It true I find people need dong. Promise them one part to give name to police. They must give three part to me. Maybe VC find these peoples and give them three part for name of me."

"You maybe need a rest. You want to leave for a couple of weeks, is that what you're leading up to?"

"No. I no want leave you."

He heard the words, but they did not really register in his consciousness. For he was compassionless, too removed to react, too isolated to understand that she was speaking from an instinct deeper than reason. So the words and their meaning passed. And he never knew.

"The VC aren't coming to Saigon. Besides, you've got the house protected. The old man made a spell and hung the mirror."

"VC will know I live here. Know I give names."

"You've got your mirror and the old soothsayer's spell."

"I have something else he give. I have protection." Rosette got up and pulled the sheet all the way to the foot of the bed. "I bring noodles for you. Cold now. But I make hot."

Plans

I

Mr. Khiem and Georges Devereaux, one of the contract
agents at Phnom Penh, thought they had a good plan. And
they did. They thought they could keep it going quietly for
many months yet, possibly years, possibly as long as the war
lasted. And they could have. If Devereaux had not gotten
a little too greedy and a little too incautious and carried a
North Vietnamese third secretary at the Embassy in Phnom
Penh as an informant even after the secretary died of syph-
ilis, and if B.D. had not gone to Cambodia to finish the
mission Fumarole had begun. But Devereaux was a little
too greedy and a little too incautious, and when B.D. found
out about it Devereaux tried to kill him, so B.D. had no
choice but to terminate Devereaux because he felt it was
right and necessary to the harmony of things. But he did it
thoroughly, as a professional should, and B.D. was a professional in every sense of the word, though he hardly ever
showed it, and nobody ever guessed it, and that was all part
of being a professional, too.

He let Devereaux live long enough to give him all the
names and places and dates before he terminated the man.
Devereaux died poorly, there was no doubt about that, but
then he was not a professional and it really did not matter,

because if he had been a professional he would never have gotten into trouble, or at least been caught. He even cried and got down on his knees. That sort of thing just was not done. But after all, what could one expect of a contract agent? The third secretary had never been their man anyway, though Khiem had certified the man as a direct source into Hanoi. B.D. had the names and the dates and the places so he shot Devereaux behind the ear with a small, very compact and very sterile pistol and made the death very swift and very painless.

B.D. got a message through to Saigon before he left Cambodia. He sent it in code through the taxi driver who drove him to Pochentong airport, and Mister Balfour ordered Khiem's detention. Knox met B.D. at the civilian side of Tan son Nhut. The Air Vietnam jet from Phnom Penh was late. Air Vietnam had only two Caravelle jets and they were very careful with them. French pilots flew them on the international runs, but they were still invariably late. It was hot, very hot, in the terminal and there were a lot of Vietnamese Army troops milling around because the benches were filled with civilians going somewhere, or just arriving, and American soldiers with PCS orders to the States sat on duffel bags or upended suitcases. The voice of a woman came over the loudspeaker and assured Knox in alternate English, Vietnamese and French that the jet from Phnom Penh would be arriving soon. Meanwhile Knox waited in the sweltering heat, bullied and reassured by the anonymous loudspeaker voice, waiting, perspiring, his crotch itching from a heat rash but not daring to scratch it, pacing, waiting, aimlessly. Threatened, cajoled and infuriated by the voice over the public-address system. And still the plane did not come.

The wait ended in the third hour. He was drinking another Ba-me-ba in the terminal restaurant and heard the Air

Vietnam jet whisper up to the deplaning area. The loudspeaker voice did not make any announcement this time,
which was customary. The woman's voice had not announced a flight correctly yet. But all the same Knox knew
it was the plane from Phnom Penh. The ground crew slid
the passenger ramps against the doors. B.D. was the last
person off the plane. He was still awkward with the cast on
his foot and a stewardess in a blue *ao dai* tried to help him
down the steps, but he shook her off. B.D. had to process
through customs, but he knew the Chief Customs Officer
and got through in a hurry. His brown suit was wrinkled,
and bagged at knees and seat. His tie was missing and his
shave and haircut somehow emanated the impression he
had been dry-cleaned instead of washed. B.D. had only an
attaché case and one small bag. Knox took them. B.D.
stumbled along with his cane, pivoting painfully and heavily
on his foot cast.

"Bad trip?" Knox said.

"Like any trip on Air Nuoc Mam," B.D. said. "You wait a
long time in a lot of places."

They got into the Embassy sedan and Knox drove toward
Saigon. A brief tropic rain squall suddenly enveloped them
and Knox turned on the wipers. They were noisy and
streaked the windshield. They did little good and he had to
drive very slowly until they reached Cach Mang because
there was a long line of petro-main trucks ahead of them.
Knox never felt very good about being behind a line of fuel
trucks. They were tempting targets for satchel charges and
a suicide team. He was glad when the trucks turned toward
Bien Hoa.

The rain had ended by the time they reached the office
but the air was still hot, still oppressive. B.D. had taken off
his coat and the shirt was tinged faintly pink where it had
touched the fine red dust collected on the seat. Normal

work hours were over and the offices were quiet, devoid of
people except the duty agent going the rounds of all the
safes. The offices seemed much larger in their silence and
emptiness.

Mister Balfour was in his office with the Negro agent
named Heaton from Los Angeles, and Khiem. Khiem was
seated in a secretary's gray swivel chair. He was strapped
in a canvas strait jacket and the sleeves were buckled to opposite ankles. He had evidently been in that position for a
long time because his forehead was wet with sweat and his
hair was matted down in places. Heaton was holding a Uzi
submachine gun loosely but competently in his hands.
Whenever he moved the muzzle still remained pointed toward Khiem.

"What did you do with Fumarole?" Mister Balfour asked
B.D.

"Some missionaries had already buried him. The legation
at Phnom Penh said nobody in the States wanted him.
Norodom gave it his personal okay."

"And Devereaux?"

"He won't ever report that he's vetted someone who
doesn't exist anymore."

"We aren't in any trouble over that, are we?" Mister Balfour asked. "You know how State feels about our even
going over there."

"No. His cover was as an archaeologist interested in the
Angor ruins. There's no way the Cambodians can link him
with us. They think the Khymer Rouge did him in."

"How long have they been doing this?"

"Hard to say. Over two years. Maybe longer."

Mister Balfour walked over to Khiem and looked at him
steadily. "You son of a bitch," he said slowly and distinctly.

Khiem did not say anything but regarded Mister Balfour
through obsidian eyes.

"You son of a bitch," Mister Balfour said again. "I trusted you." Then to no one in particular: "That's a lot of IIRs with false information. A lot of reports going back to Washington without any facts other than opium dreams concocted by this fucking bastard."

"Nobody reads them anyway," B.D. said. "Most of them find their way to the classified trash in short order."

"They're still IIRs we put out. We've got our ass in a sling; just think of all the work that'll have to be done in Washington to purge the system of false reports. All our reports are going into a computer now, you know."

"Damn right, I know," B.D. said. "Takes twice as long to type one when you have to put all those numbers on every frigging sheet of paper."

"Tell me," Khiem spoke for the first time since Knox and B.D. had entered the room. "How did you find out? I ask this to satisfy my curiosity only."

"That's none of your affair," Mister Balfour said. "We did and that was the end of the scheme."

"Was it because of the Frenchman's greed?"

No one replied. Khiem took this silence for assent. "That was it. The French are too grasping. I worked for them a long time. I know."

"What do we do with him now?" Heaton asked.

"We terminate him," Mister Balfour said.

"Don't you want to get some information out of him?"

"No."

"Then why not turn him over to the National Police?" Heaton said. "Why dirty our hands with him?"

"No," Mister Balfour said fiercely. "And let them know we were buying false information? Not on your life."

"That is precisely why you will spare mine," Khiem said.

"You're wrong on that point," Mister Balfour said.

"I am a long-time worker with the French SDECE and I

have worked for you. You are not so naive as to think I would not have a policy of assurance in a safe place."

"You're not that smart," Mister Balfour said. "You're a slope and you're greedy."

Khiem blinked his eyes for a moment but let the name pass. "Perhaps I am not as you Occidentals, but nevertheless I have taken certain precautions. I have made copies of all payments given out to agents who never exist. All the worthless information I made up and you bought. Even your replies to such information. I make it to agree with what you want to hear. I made several copies of each paper on your excellent Xerox machine."

"That's a good bluff but it just won't wash."

"As you say. Then I suggest you get on with the troublesome of eliminating me. I am certain you will be able to think of an appropriate explanation for your superiors before details of how badly you were duped become known to the press. You will find my copies in a certain place in my house. Please inform yourself as to the truthfulness of my speaking and judge the damage your government will suffer."

"He's not as dumb as you might think, Chief," B.D. said. "We should check it out."

"That'll take too long," Mister Balfour said. "I'm due at a party Loan's giving at eight tonight. I want this thing settled by then."

"If he's telling the truth we're in deep shit," Heaton said. "That kind of information would really be embarrassing to CAS if what Khiem says is true and some newspaper gets a hold of it."

Khiem smiled. "That is a thing your Mr. Helms would not like."

"All right." Mister Balfour pointed at B.D. then at Heaton. "You two go see what this bastard has at his house.

Rip it apart if you have to. I think Knox and I can watch one fucking Vietnamese."

B.D. asked Khiem where the papers were and Khiem said they were in the bottom of a clothes wardrobe in his bedroom. They left, and Knox sat in Mister Balfour's office. Heaton had given him the Uzi and he moved to a straight chair and watched Khiem. Mister Balfour sat at his desk and signed outgoing cablegrams. He also looked at his watch every two minutes.

Khiem sat in the swivel chair and was very uncomfortable. "Would you be kind enough to adjust my bindings?" he asked. "They are most tight."

"No," Mister Balfour said.

"You are only increasing the price you will have to pay," Khiem said. He sounded very resigned.

Mister Balfour did not say anything. They continued to sit in the office with the strain and the discomfort, though it was a different kind of strain and discomfort for each of them.

B.D. and Heaton had a strain of their own, a half-hour's drive across Saigon in heavy traffic of evening, and a half-hour's drive back, but they returned as soon as they could make it in the heat and the traffic and the people, and they had three heavy office folders with expansion sides when they came in. The folders were filled with thick stacks of copy paper, and B.D. put them on Mister Balfour's desk without comment. His jaws were working silently.

Mister Balfour removed some papers from one folder and read the papers on top of one stack; then sorted through the other stacks at random. The room was silent except for the turning of the pages. He read for what seemed to be a long time and did not once look at his watch, though it was really not very long at all. "How many copies of this do you have?"

"I have only the one copy. But others have enough copies."

"You can be made to talk. Blackmailers are the easiest kind of people to break."

"Not when they have something very precious to protect. To me my life is very precious."

"I'm asking you for the last time, how many copies did you make and who has them?"

"I cannot tell you."

"Did you get any information on this from Devereaux?" Mister Balfour said to B.D.

B.D. shook his head. "I doubt if Devereaux knew Khiem was making copies."

"He was unaware of it," Khiem said. "All he cared about was the money. Had he been more cautious he may have taken policy of assurance as I have."

Mister Balfour got up from his desk and walked to the swivel chair where Khiem was strapped and spun him around. He kept spinning the chair and trying to make it go faster but Khiem's knees kept bumping against the chair base. He stopped Khiem and slapped him as hard as he could across the mouth. The blow brought no blood, but the imprint of his hand lingered vividly on Khiem's mouth for a long time.

Mister Balfour struck him again. Khiem turned his cheek. The blow broke skin this time and a thin line of blood appeared in the seam of his lips. Mister Balfour started to strike the man again, but B.D. caught his hand. "Rough stuff won't work, Chief. This bastard won't talk if you beat him within an inch of hell. Let's call in the guy with the little black bag."

Mister Balfour bit his lower lip and looked at his watch. "You mean Hines. I don't want to get any more people involved in this. I think maybe I can cover it up."

"It's the only way we can get Khiem to talk. You can kick the truth out of a Vietnamese only if you've got some sort of hold over him. Khiem's got nothing to lose but his life. You've got Hines, may as well use him."

"All right. Go get Hines up here and tell him to bring plenty of Pentothal."

"I'll get him," B.D. said. "Heaton, you and Knox open a slit in that jacket so we can get a needle into him. Better yet, put him on the Chief's desk. Stretch him out so he's as loose as possible." Heaton put the compact Uzi submachine gun across a chair. Together he and Knox bundled Khiem over to the desk. Mister Balfour cleared the top of papers. He sat down in the corner to read some more of the documents Khiem had reproduced. They stretched Khiem on the desk and tied the sleeve straps to the desk legs.

B.D. was back in ten minutes with a tall, spare man who had a head like a pumpkin. The man carried a physician's medical kit and chewed gum constantly. This was Hines. Knox had never seen him before. Hines tipped Khiem's chin back and looked at his pupils. Khiem twisted his head to one side and Hines grasped a shock of hair and held him steady until he was satisfied. "He's a good subject, strong enough to stand it." Hines looked at the slit Knox had made in the upper sleeve of the strait jacket. It was not long enough so he tried to rip it with his fingers, but the canvas was too heavy so he took a scalpel from his kit. Khiem started to thrash about in the strait jacket and Hines quickly jerked the scapel away so he would not cut the man. "You'd better tie his feet," Hines said. He dug through the medical bag and handed Knox a roll of adhesive tape. Heaton held Khiem's feet together and Knox taped them.

B.D. and Heaton held Khiem for a while, but B.D.'s ankle was hurting badly so he yielded his place to Knox. Khiem struggled briefly even though his legs were bound, but his captors were stronger than he, so he stopped struggling and let them do with him as they wished. Hines twisted a length of rubber tubing about Khiem's bicep, extra tight because of the canvas and because he knew Khiem would not make a fist. He carefully inserted a syringe through the slit and probed with it until he aspirated blood. Then he loosened the tourniquet and pressed the plunger of the syringe slightly. Khiem struggled as the drug stung him.

"Hold him absolutely steady," Hines said.

"How long is this Pentothal going to take?" Mister Balfour was looking at his watch again. He had put aside the papers.

"It's not Pentothal," Hines said without turning his head. "It's better, sort of a synthetic scopoline with something extra to really relax the subconscious. But you've really got to be careful how fast you give it; otherwise, you'll overload the nervous system."

"I've got a party to attend. Make it as fast as you can."

Hines did not reply. Khiem was relaxing visibly and Hines sat on the edge of the desk. Knox and Heaton were still holding Khiem's legs and shoulders. Hines put a finger on Khiem's neck to feel the pulse and slowly pushed in more of the drug. "What do you want to ask him?" Hines said. "He's under good now." He lifted Khiem's eyelid with one thumb and peered closely at the pupil.

"Wait a minute, get the recorder set up." Mister Balfour pointed to a low cabinet behind his desk. "We can't risk bringing in a secretary to take it down."

"Be damn quick. I've got to watch this stuff real close or it'll kill him."

Mister Balfour looked at B.D. B.D. had set up the recorder and tapped the microphone several times in approved fashion to make sure the signal would be clear. He nodded.

"Ask him how many copies he made of the documents involving the false North Vietnamese sources. Ask him who has the other copies and where they are."

"One at a time, one at a time," Hines said. He was very cool and very sure of himself. He was also irritating the hell out of Mister Balfour, but there was nothing Mister Balfour could do about it because Hines was very cool and very sure of himself and he apparently knew his job. Hines rephrased the question. "Mister Khiem, the papers you made. How many copies did you make? The ones with the false information."

Khiem paused for a moment. He hawked, then swallowed some phlegm. Then he began speaking very slowly and dreamily, but very clearly. They could see the drug had taken effect. He spoke in Vietnamese.

"Sweet Jesus Christ," Mister Balfour said. "Tell him to answer in English."

Hines held up a cautionary hand and repeated the question, then told Khiem to reply in English. Khiem answered in Vietnamese. Hines asked the question several times; each time he lost a little of his cool, a little of his professional detachment. Khiem continued to answer in Vietnamese.

"It's no use," Hines said. "He isn't going to answer in English."

"Translate what he's saying then, goddamn it."

"I can't speak Vietnamese," Hines said. The corners of his lips were twitching and he was in danger of losing his cool and detached professionalism.

"What do you do when you shoot that stuff into other Vietnamese?"

"I have a translator. Sometimes I used Khiem."

Mister Balfour swore profusely. He was using words Knox had never heard. Finally Mister Balfour subsided. He paced to a small mirror in the corner above his washbasin and began knotting a tie. "Then get another man in here. Fuck, what difference does it make if the whole frigging world knows? The rate we're going we might as well bring in the whole office."

"I should have thought of this before and had someone here," B.D. said.

"No, Hines should have thought of it and gotten an interpreter."

"Just a minute now," Heaton said. "We can't risk bringing in a Vietnamese interpreter."

"Then get the person who speaks Vietnamese the best."

"We'll have to get somebody from the Embassy," B.D. said. "None of our people are that good."

Mister Balfour was quite resigned now. He had knotted his tie and his composure. He spoke in the same tenor of voice throughout. "Then get somebody from the Embassy over here. Lay off the Pentothal for now." He inclined his head at Knox. "You're coming to the dinner with me. I'm supposed to bring someone. I was going to take B.D., give him a rest after all the work he did in Cambodia, but I want him to run this show while I'm gone."

"You think I'm not capable of running it," Hines said.

"That's exactly what I think," Mister Balfour said.

Hines did not say anything in reply.

"I'm not wearing a tie," said Knox.

"That doesn't matter. You'll do for short notice." Mister Balfour led the way to the door. "Keep the tape. I'll listen to it later. If you find out he's lying about those extra copies, then I don't want to see him when I return."

II

The dinner was excellent and General Loan served Cantonese duckling with bamboo shoots (flown in from Da Lat,

very tender and very young) as well as two different kinds
of pork. There were two kinds of rice, too, the long-grained
delta rice and some of the IR-8 strain in a curry. Even in a
curry the IR-8 was hard and tasteless. But since Thieu had
said he liked IR-8 the USAID rice was served at every State
occasion. So Loan served it, too, but everyone ate the delta
rice. Even the USAID people who were there.

Loan sat at the head of the table. He was wearing freshly
laundered fatigues with the sleeves rolled up. Mister Balfour was the only one wearing a tie, and when he thought
no one was looking he took it off. The party was in honor of
a senior USAID adviser to the National Police Department
of Public Safety and Internal Security who was returning to
the States the following day. He made a short speech later
on, and some of the other USAID advisers gave Loan a
small short-barreled .38 caliber Smith and Wesson revolver
as a Tet gift. But by then the Vietnamese were talking
among themselves, and some of the Americans were drunk,
so no one really heard the speech, and that was just as
well.

Knox sat down the table from Mister Balfour, past the
middle and across from a National Police major. The major
had been present at the street demonstration in front of Gia
Long Palace. He did not recognize Knox. The major was
eating with chopsticks. Knox was using a battered knife
and fork left over from the colonial period. From time to
time waiters in short white coats which were relatively
clean changed dishes or brought in more food. They were
much more efficient than the waiters in the local restaurants. Knox said as much to the National Police major.

"Thank you," the National Police major said. "We train
them. VC make good server boy you think."

Knox put down his fork. "They're VC?"

"But of yes. VC. They grow also the food. We have an

island that way from here." The major pointed vaguely toward the south with his chopsticks. "They grow much pig
and duck and cook for us. Very nice arrangements but of
yes."

"But of yes," Knox said. "Aren't you afraid, though, they
might try to escape? What if they should try to poison your
food?"

He had to ask the question twice to get the National Police major to understand him. The major laid his chopsticks
on the tablecloth. "If they try to do that thing you say we
kill them. They are happy to work for us. Most better than
VC in jungle. But we kill them if they try to poison us." The
major picked up his chopsticks and selected a sliver of bamboo
shoot. He chewed it very slowly and smiled at Knox in his
wisdom and vast unshakable humor which no Occidental
could ever hope to understand.

Knox and Mister Balfour left early. Mister Balfour pled
an early appointment the following morning, and Loan let
them go after Mister Balfour had two stiff drinks of Scotch
in honor of the departing USAID adviser. Mister Balfour
promptly went to sleep when they got into the sedan. Knox
concentrated on maneuvering the big car through the
poorly lighted streets. The American military curfew was
about to begin and soldiers in pedicabs and taxis were
hurrying past them on their way to their billets.

The party had been held in a National Police safe house
on a very narrow alley and while they were inside the house
someone had scraped the side of the sedan so there was a
long scar in the paint on the driver's side. But Knox did not
mention that and hoped Mister Balfour would not notice it.
He had never said anything about the jeep step. Loan had
given Mister Balfour a bottle of Scotch at the door. It was
very good Scotch and it still had the A&AFES stamp on the
label. When you were a National Policeman, especially

when you were the Director General, you did not have to bother with cutting out the stamp. Loan had a case of Scotch by the door and he had given bottles to all the important guests. Knox had not gotten one. Mister Balfour's bottle was between them on the seat and it almost rolled off the seat when Knox braked hard to avoid a cyclo which shot out from a side street. He put it in the glove compartment when he parked the car in the guarded courtyard behind the CAS Headquarters. The Nung guard saw him put the bottle away, then waken Mister Balfour. The Nung went over later, several hours later, after everyone had gone, when all the lights in the building were out, and removed the bottle of Scotch from the glove compartment. But Mister Balfour had already forgotten about the Scotch and Knox never thought to mention it. The Nung guard traded it two days later for one kilo of delta rice and a flyblown fish.

III

Khiem was strapped in the swivel chair again, as he had been when Knox first came in with B.D. that afternoon. That seemed a long time ago. Now it was almost midnight. Khiem looked very strained. His face was pale and the canvas strait jacket was dark with perspiration even though the air conditioner was turned up full force. The office was cloudy with cigarette smoke. B.D. was sitting in Mister Balfour's chair which he had rolled from behind the desk. He had his foot with the cast on it resting in another chair. There was another man, a stranger whom Knox had never seen before, though he knew the man was from the Embassy. Hines was not in the office but his doctor's bag was still on Mister Balfour's desk.

"I see he's still alive," Mister Balfour said. He massaged

at the sleep in his eyes with thumb and forefinger.

B.D. did not get up from his chair. His eyes were puffy from the acrid smoke and lack of sleep. He looked almost as strained as Khiem. "He's made six copies of everything. He says people in Hong Kong, Manila, oh yes, and Phnom Penh have them. These people will turn the documents over to third-country newspapermen if they don't get certain letters from him within a certain time."

"Did he give you the substance of the messages?"

"Yes, he told us that, but the messages must be in his own handwriting. I don't think we can get him to write the letters."

Mister Balfour sat down on the corner of the desk. "Something he picked up from the SDECE. They do things like that. You have their names, these people in Hong Kong and Phom Penh?"

"He gave us their names. Addresses too. The people in Hong Kong and Manila are ordinary merchants. Vietnamese businessmen in the export trade. The man in Phnom Penh is very close to people in Sihanouk's government, though."

"Give me a cigarette," Mister Balfour said. B.D. gave him his pack. Knox had never seen Mister Balfour smoke. There was not even an ashtray in the office and B.D. was using a paper cup which had once held coffee. The dregs of coffee were still in the cup and they were stained a dirty gray with the wet ash. The first time B.D. had taken Knox in to meet Mister Balfour B.D. had used an empty cigarette pack for an ashtray. Mister Balfour smoked the cigarette down to the filter and pinched it out with his fingers. No one said anything for a long time.

"How much do you want?" He said at length.

Khiem smiled. "First you must release me from this restraint."

"No deal. You can talk just as well from where you are. Now. Give me your price."

"Five hundret thousan dollars for not disclosing the information. Ten thousan dollars for each time you hit me. That is five hundret and twenty thousan American dollars to be deposited to my name to Hong Kong bank."

"That is too much."

"That is the only price I will make. It is not negotiable."

"I do not intend to negotiate with you. If I give you the money you will only ask for more. We are both in a bad spot. I don't particularly want the word spread around that we were duped into buying false information. Most particularly since one of our own agents was involved in it. And one of our interpreters. The head interpreter at that. Though Devereaux was only a contract agent and we could probably say he was working for someone else. But if I let you go you could still give the papers to newsmen. You can still blackmail CAS for more money, any time you felt like it. That puts us in a very compromised position."

Khiem's expression did not change. He was self-assured, triumphant, like most Vietnamese. He was still contemptuous. "The French paid. Your predecessor paid. They were glad to pay. It is an old game. The SDECE was trapped, the man before you was trapped. I was smarter than them all. Your predecessor paid one million dollars. I got only small part of it because someone else was it who caught your man with false papers. He thought he was lucky."

Mister Balfour rolled the cigarette filter between his fingers critically. "I know my predecessor let himself be blackmailed. That's why he's not here any longer. That's why I'm here instead of him right now." He flicked the filter at Khiem, but Khiem saw the cigarette filter in time and turned his head. "Are you sure you have the names of these people, particularly the one in Cambodia?" he said to the man from the Embassy.

"Yes, I have all the names and addresses. I wrote them down, but they are on the tape as well. You can listen to that if you like."

"No. I have confidence in you. Only you must not tell anyone, not even friends among your own people, what you have heard tonight."

The man nodded. Mister Balfour thanked him and the man from the Embassy left without looking back. Mister Balfour turned to Khiem. "You're a condom," He said. He spoke very matter-of-factly and seemed to believe what he was saying. "A condom is something you use only once for a particular job. Then you discard it. It's usually a cheap, messy job when you don't altogether like to get involved. Then when you're through you toss it away without a thought."

Khiem was contemptuous still. "You may call me anything you like, it will only cost you more money. You cannot get rid of me without a lot of unpleasantness appearing to you. You think I did not know about your drugs. Remember, I was with Hines when he questioned other Vietnamese. I have a precaution for that."

Mister Balfour had been rummaging through Hines's medical bag. He was doing it quietly so Khiem would not hear him. He found what he was looking for and held up a large syringe. He began to fill it from a vial of the synthetic scopoline. He held the bottle upside down and inserted the needle through the rubber diaphragm, then holding the barrel of the syringe in the palm of one hand with the vial he drew back on the plunger with his other hand. He knew how to fill a syringe properly. Khiem was facing away from the desk. He was still talking. "Your words are like the French. They are empty. Which is good for you since you must swallow them. The French were glad to pay. I was easy to trick them about the Viet Minh. They lost many men and I made much, much money. They were even happy to give me the recommendation to you. But I have my honor. I do not speak of those matters after they paid me."

"You mean once you're bought you stay bought."

"Yes, you have my words."

"I think you're lying about your precaution. I don't believe you thought we'd go that far. I believe you thought we'd fold up and pay you before that." Then to B.D.: "You have those names. Do you think you can get close to them in time?" Mister Balfour was standing behind Khiem's chair. The syringe lay in his hand, the needle back along his wrist, like a dart, so Khiem could not see it.

B.D. nodded. "It may take nearly as much as he's asking to get the papers from the man in Cambodia. But I can get next to him."

"Then it's your project," Mister Balfour said. He thrust the needle into Khiem's kidney from behind, stooping slightly to do it, and stabbing through the canvas of the jacket. Khiem tensed in his chair. The veins of his neck bulged and purpled as he tried to speak, but paralysis had seized him. A thrust to the kidneys always did that. It was an old assassin's trick. He injected all the serum, then whipped out the syringe and leaned across to whisper something in Khiem's ear, but nobody else heard what he said.

Part of the paralysis wore off and Khiem began to wail in low, choking tones. Heaton covered Khiem's mouth with his hand. Khiem's mouth closed involuntarily and his body convulsed. But Heaton stopped the cry and after about a minute Khiem stopped struggling. Mister Balfour helped Heaton pry his finger from Khiem's mouth. Heaton's finger was bleeding profusely. Mister Balfour gave him his handkerchief and Heaton wrapped the handkerchief around his finger and Mister Balfour tied a knot with the ends.

"Get this son of a bitch over to the National Interrogation Center. Give him a hand," he said to Knox. "Tell the people at the center that the VC knew Khiem was working for us and they killed him. Poisoned him. I'll call ahead and ask them to dispose of the body for us. Thank God he doesn't have any family. Otherwise we'd have to tell them he was a hero and give them a few thousand piastres."

Knox and Heaton began untying the strait jacket. Mister Balfour took a cigarette from B.D.'s pack which was still on his desk. B.D. pushed the desk chair back to its usual position and Mister Balfour sat down. "Stop by and see if Hines is still in his office," he said to Heaton. "If he is get a shot for that bite. You never know what sort of germs those fucking Vietnamese may have."

"Watch those cigarettes, Chief, they rot your lungs, you always tell me that." Mister Balfour ignored B.D. and B.D. took a cigarette for himself. Mister Balfour tried to light his cigarette but his hand was unsteady and B.D. took the lighter and held it for him.

"Do you think I did the right thing?" he asked B.D. He was like an infantryman who showed great courage in combat, on the battlefield in front of bullets, but gave up when the combat was over. He was overcome by the enormity of his daring and courage had deserted him.

"I don't know if you did the right thing," B.D. said. "You did the only thing. You'd better sign some vouchers now so I can get some money first thing in the morning. I've got to get back to Cambodia or the shit'll really be all over the fan."

Tet Nguyen Dan

I

THE WEEK BEFORE, National Police and Army CID agents had raided all the bookstores on Tu Do Street. They carried off a lot of ledgers with American names, dates and amounts of money converted. The Army and Air Force investigators were systematically opening cases on the people identified, and no Vietnamese would change money with an American unless he had done business with the man before. All the Indian tailors were staying out of sight; they had not been raided, but all the same they closed their shops and waited. A lot of Americans were running scared.

The Army arrested an ex-officer who was reputed to be the biggest moneychanger in Saigon, and he was giving the CID a lot of names, too, in promise of amnesty. Three Army deserters living above bars with their girl friends surrendered to MP posts because there was a rumor the Viet Cong were going to strike and strike hard during Tet. That was a rumor the intelligence services had been hearing for over a month now, and just as dutifully they had been publishing IIRs and special reports about alleged Viet Cong build-ups around Saigon. But as always the IIRs and special reports were late and the people who received them were too harassed with the petty tasks of running a war and getting over to the exchange to see if another shipment of Japanese tape recorders had come in to read the IIRs and special reports. Besides that, the people writing the IIRs did not believe the reports anyway. No one even bothered to report the fears of the three deserters. They were trucked off to the stockade at LBJ to await courts-martial.

The Vietnamese Army had given certain units permission to go to half strength for the Tet, and though the Americans were saying they were ready for anything, they were relaxing somewhat because, after all, a truce of sorts had been arranged. MACV announced a special early curfew for American military personnel, and let it go at that.

The Chinese moneychangers in Cholon were not taking any new business, but the raids had the effect of drying up the supply of green, so that the price of green almost doubled in four days. It was a seller's market if you had the green, but Calvin Davies was worried. He summoned a meeting with some pilots from Air America, two Army sergeants who had been in Vietnam for two years because they had soft jobs at MACV and had discovered the market during their first six months, a French former colon with a wooden leg he had acquired during some insignificant, long-forgotten skirmish over control of the Michelin plantation. And Knox.

II

They met at the Loan Mai Hotel, six floors, bar on the roof. Small elevated dancing area where the bargirls danced with each other to cheap music from a stolen juke box until some American asked one of them for a dance and they could con him for a tea afterward. One hundred p for a Coke, ice in large chunks with small bits of debris clinging to it, a good view of the city, with modern conveniences — if you believed the advertising — bargirls, some in Western dress, some in *ao dias*, just as in any other bar, talking to men, officers, enlisted, black, white, RMK civilians. Trying anything for a tea.

And if you stayed until the bar closed at 2300 and went downstairs, you found girls in the hallways with the one thing and the one thing only in mind. Trying to get you to take them in for a trick or the night. Expensive girls, girls with consummate skills at fellatio and other more mystic acts, *nha ques* only a week from the hamlet with absolutely no skills and a deep sense of guilt, who had not eaten in three days and who hoped to entice enough from the easier marks for at least one meal. They were so ubiquitous and so evident, lining the stairs on both sides, even squatting in the hallways (the *nha ques* did; the older, smarter girls had long ago learned not to squat) that young men, virgins in their own right, sometimes felt embarrassed and sorry for them and gave them small piastre bills. Sometimes they gave the bills to the wrong women, the expensive ones, and they threw the money away in disgust. But one of the others always caught it.

Knox walked to the hotel in the late-January afternoon. He had driven B.D. to the airport an hour earlier and he wished he could have kept the staff car. There were few taxis on the streets. Tet was in progress with a vengeance and the taxi drivers were celebrating, too. The streets were crowded with dragon floats and children throwing firecrackers. The battle-hardened veterans of Dak To, Operation Junction City, Pershing and a dozen other campaigns lived through but remembered only because they were alive shuddered, for the pop of firecrackers was indistinguishable from small arms fire. And raised the hair in back of scalps with a prickle brought by increased adrenalin, as they watched warily out the doors of billets. But the Tu Do commandos did not know the difference between gunfire and firecrackers and moved about, oblivious to everything but their own sharply defined desires and appetites.

The streets were bright with noise and heavy with the pungency of *nuoc mam*. Garish with the fortunate colors of red and gold; pots of kumquat plants, good luck symbols, flourished on street corners. Impromptu shops selling sweetmeats and Tet confections competed for space on sidewalks with bicycle repair stalls. Old men, working in front of buildings, were hanging Tet banners while other old men labored with calligraphy to paint still more banners with delicate brush strokes, and callipygian young girls fanned freshly lighted joss sticks with conical hats until the incense smoldered to their satisfaction and they celebrated their birthdays and Buddha's simultaneously.

Knox found it best to walk close to the walls of buildings. There were less people and he was out of the way, though the scant open spaces did attract firecrackers and a fistfight over candy stolen from an old woman. But he could maintain a steady pace except when snapping firecrackers nipped at his ankles. He arrived at the Loan Mai before Davies. Knox waited in the cramped lobby for fifteen minutes until he saw Davies drive up and park in the hotel parking lot. Davies had bought a stolen jeep and had it painted black. Air America and ConAir both had jeeps procured from the big salvage yard at Go Vap and painted black, so no one gave Davies a second glance, except possibly to envy him for having a jeep.

Davies had two people with him. Knox had never seen them before. They were the two Air America pilots and they were dressed like Knox in Saigon fatigues. Davies locked the jeep's steering wheel and nodded to Knox. He led the way to the elevator and Knox followed. He was coldly furious with Davies. He would be even more dismayed when the two Army sergeants and the Frenchman arrived. He stood close beside Davies as the two Air America pilots went out onto the roof. "I thought this was to be just you and me," he said, but Davies ignored him.

They took a table by the edge of the roof so the cool of the evening would be more apparent. And their words less apt to be overheard. After a while the Army sergeants came up. One of them looked like a tall baby, with transparent skin and a helmet of milkweed-pod hair. The other sergeant had a bottle of gin and a fifth of cheap bourbon in crinkled paper sacks. They ordered ice and mixes. Knox asked for a Ba-me-ba. They drank in silence, feeling each other's presence near against them, though nothing was said until the Frenchman arrived. Knox watched the bargirls hustling the Americans, but they did not try to hustle the Frenchman when he walked over to join them. He got there just at sundown. He was dressed in a faded gingham shirt with the tails out for coolness, and he had a spade beard. His limp was detectable only if you knew he had a wooden leg and listened for the tiny, scarcely audible *snap-snap* of the metal joint where once he had a kneecap. He raised an eyebrow when he saw the other people. He had not been expecting anyone but Davies either.

Introductions were made. They sat together uneasily. The Frenchman refused a drink. Finally Davies said: "We've got our tails in a crack. The police are closing down a lot of moneychangers. MACV has a computer and it's going to be used to keep track of all money orders sold to military personnel."

"That's not going to affect us," the sergeant with the fair

hair said. "We're not dealing through any of the people the CID picked up."

"No, it hasn't affected us yet, but it's starting to get hot. I got us all here together to discuss branching out into other lines." Davies looked at the Frenchman. "All of us except you are changing money. You're running gold and opium. We'd like to buy into your business."

"Hold it," the taller of the two Air America pilots said. "I didn't come along to buy into any opium racket. I didn't bargain for any of that."

"Quiet," the second Air America pilot said. "There're rumors the scrip is going to change. Just like the Army did in Korea, change the series quick, then bang, change it again a couple of weeks later. If we want to keep socking away some coin we'd better think about getting into something else."

"So the MPC changes. The money boys in Cholon will be offering us four to one to take MPC off their hands."

"Yes," the one-legged Frenchman said. "You are right, unless you cannot get rid of the MPC in time. Then you have a lot of useless paper you can't change into your fine green money."

"You picked a hell of a place to discuss this," Knox said.

"Keep your voice down," Davies said. "This is the last place anybody'd think we were having a meeting like this. What could be more harmless than a group of old friends having a drink?"

"I say it wasn't too smart. It's not very smart for these people to see me. That could make things sticky."

"And I said keep your voice down," Davies's voice was hard and brittle but his lips were smiling in case anyone chanced to look their way. "We're not smalltime any longer. There're more people involved in this thing than you'll ever know. We've got to plan ahead to the time when it won't be profitable to change money and we'll need something else."

"If he wants out so badly," one sergeant said, "let him out. I'd rather not have him."

"Shut up, all of you. Nobody gets out. We're all in this ass deep."

"Not me." Knox pushed back his chair and stood up.

"Sit down," Davies said.

"I'm going."

"I said sit down. You'll cause a scene. And you're the one who wants to avoid calling attention to himself."

Knox sat down reluctantly.

Davies continued. "There's maybe six, eight months of profitability left in this war from the moneychanging angle. We've got to branch out into something with potential, and that something's opium running, with maybe some gold smuggling on the side."

"I agree with your friend," the more cautious of the Air America pilots said to Davies. "We've all made money. Let's stop now before we get crapped on."

"He's right, Davies. It's lasted too long. We've been goddamned lucky," said Knox.

"And I tell you we can still grease it. We've got too much at stake. Besides," Davies said very matter-of-factly, "you have no choice."

One of the sergeants stooped to retie a bootlace. They were both wearing jungle fatigues and canvas-sided boots. Even though neither of them had been farther from Saigon than the PX at Cholon. "You think there's money in this smuggling business."

"Yes. I ran into a fellow a while back. Australian. Poses as a banker and flies all over the world. He's a courier for Viets who want to get their money out of this fucking place.

The point is, he showed me how's to do it. We buy the gold here for cash and arrange deposit anywhere the customers want. The Viets get a wad stowed away in some bank account, and we take the gold to Hong Kong and sell it for a pretty stiff price."

"Please allow yourself some elaboration about the scheme for gold." The Frenchman said. "I may be interested. But it will depend upon your terms."

"I'm against it," the cautious Air America pilot said.

But Davies began to discuss the scheme and everyone huddled over the table in dense conspiracy, except Knox and the one Air America pilot. Knox sat in hopeless rage. For he had discovered that seeking pleasure and avoiding pain eventually led to impasses. Then he discovered it was not so much an obstacle to be faced and hence overcome, therefore solved, but a Damoclean sword of peril under which he labored with no idea of how to extricate himself. He had never weighed decisions in terms of consequences, though consequences followed and flowed from decisions and he had no one to blame for those consequences. Except, of course, himself.

So they sat and talked. About gold and green currency, and opium too, and how they were going to make other fortunes, plans grandiose and banal; waxing enthusiastic, drinking; Knox sitting slumped in his chair, one hand half-shielding his face as if to avoid recognition. Several times Davies asked him if he had anything to say, and each time Knox shook his head mutely. The others were fairly well ignoring him and he liked that, though he wished there was some way he could leave; it was late and he wanted to get back to Rosette. The two sergeants were becoming restive. It was almost curfew time. Davies did not notice.

A lot of firecrackers were exploding in the street. They all heard them, but had long since relegated the sounds to insignificance. Tet had always been noisy, the Frenchman said. Knox's eyes began to droop. He nodded from time to time. He no longer followed the conversation. He sat dark and secretive within himself, nursing his shame and resentment, the talk from the men at the table nothing more than a drowsy murmur. He plotted how he would triumph over Davies, humiliate him. Decisively. He imagined himself in several situations in which Davies was humbled. He rejected them because he feared Davies. He hated Davies, but he feared him more.

The first mortar round was a big one. It was close, too. Perhaps it was even a rocket, not one of the big 122-millimeter Russian rockets (which it took two men to carry and were launched from their packing crates that converted into a simple ramp, much simpler than anything the Americans had), but big enough. The concussion rocked everyone on the terrace. Their table collapsed and fragments of rusty tin from the roof filtered down. The concussion was followed by another, even closer. The lights went out and the women on the roof began screaming. The firecrackers started up again, only this time they did not sound innocuous. The hotel seemed to writhe like a living thing when the concussion waves from the third explosion hit it. Knox was thrown to the floor. Someone stepped on his hand. He was lying in a pool of broken glass and beer. No doubt about it, they were rockets. His ears rang from the blasts and he could hear nothing. He saw the lazy arc of machine-gun tracers float up from the direction of Cholon and fall soundlessly into the center of Saigon. The ringing abated somewhat and he could hear confused voices.

The lights flickered on for an instant, but that was all. Knox's eyes adjusted to the darkness and he continued to lie on the floor because he did not know what else to do. A vague figure tripped over him, fell, cursed, and stumbled away in a different direction, toward the railing. But the railing was no longer around the edge of the terrace. The bulk paused for a moment, outlined against the faint sky, feet still moving as if walking forward, then arms began flailing the unsupporting air. The bulk vanished abruptly. There was not even a cry to mark the place where it had been.

"Jesuschrist," Knox heard someone say. He realized it was Davies. Only the voice was high pitched, one octave below outright panic. "Who was that?"

"I think one of the Army sergeants," the Frenchman said. Knox could not locate him in the dark. Something like dry rice pouring into a pan hissed against the metal roof. Bright specks of tracer glimmered briefly. Then were gone. Someone else cried out in terror. The cry came up from somewhere deep in the bowels, a lusty cry of dread and despond. Then it was choked off quickly, as if cut by a knife. "Let's get off the roof."

"Who's firing at us?"

"The VC, idiot. It is a bad one, really bad. Let us get some walls between us and those bullets."

Davies began crawling cautiously across the floor. The Frenchman followed. He was not really crawling. His artificial leg would not permit that. He lay on his side and pushed himself along with his hands. He made good progress that way, too, except he could not see where he was going and kept colliding with tables. Knox followed the Frenchman. He kept his head down and did not look up. He was guided by the sounds the Frenchman made and felt very very carefully before him for broken glass. They reached the door to the staircase, and it was locked. Two Vietnamese bargirls were beating feebly at the door and whimpering. They could all see better now. There were a lot of tracers in the air and the big rockets were still coming in, mortars too, but they were passing over the Loan Mai and landing further into Saigon. The noise was almost bearable now.

Davies pushed the girls away. "Open the goddamn door," he shouted. His voice was hoarse but he had possession of himself again. The door remained closed. "Open the goddamn door or I'll kick the sonofabitch off the mother fuckin' hinges."

They waited a moment, then "All right, break it down, we got to get off this roof."

Knox and one of the Air America pilots threw their weight against the door. It groaned, and they hit it again. This time it sagged on its hinges and the third time they hit it the door broke in the middle. They were frantic and possessed of a strength they never knew they had. They hurled themselves against the door, and either the door or their shoulders would have given on the fourth attempt. The Air America pilot flashed his lighter. Davies knocked it out of his hand.

"Why the shit you do that?" the Air America pilot said. He was very frightened. Almost as frightened as Knox.

"Fuckin' idiot, want to draw some fire up here?"

"We got to see where we're going."

"You're out of your screwing tree, Davies," the remaining Army sergeant said. "There're whole buildings burning out there. Nobody's going to shoot at one little cigarette lighter."

"Okay, let's have a light. Knox, you got a light?"

"Permit me," the Frenchman said. He thumbed his lighter into flame. The light was small, they could not even see each other in its dim bronze circle. They could see the stairs, though, and they had a rallying point. The Frenchman put a hand against the wall and began to descend the stairs. He took short, abrupt steps, putting both feet on the same step before descending another. The only sounds they heard now were their breathing and the soft *snap-snap* of the Frenchman's metal knee.

Other people were behind them now, other people who had been trapped on the roof. But they were quiet. One of the bargirls behind Knox put a hand on his shoulder. He did not shrug it off. He felt very exposed. Vulnerable. Faces floated into the flaring circle of light. They were at the first landing. Five bus boys were huddled together, eyes wide in high-cheeked terror, too numb to go any farther, perhaps able to run a few yards more if kicked, but as spellbound by fear as a sparrow held by the gaze of a cobra. They stumbled over the bus boys and reversed directions to descend further. The rest of the people from the roof followed them, tripping over the bus boys in their turn.

The Frenchman cursed. "Somebody give me a handkerchief. This lighter is hot." He shifted the lighter to his other hand and blew on his fingers. Knox gave him his handkerchief. The Frenchman wrapped the handkerchief around the base of the lighter and they descended to another landing.

There was light below them now. The harsh, shadowless, colorless glare of gasoline under pressure. They could go faster: they were getting closer to the bottom, and the source of light. Which was provident because the Frenchman's lighter spluttered and went out. He tried to light it again, but the lighter was out of fluid. He shook it a few times to cool it, then put it in his pocket, still wrapped in Knox's handkerchief.

The front entrance was closed and chairbacks had been placed under the doorknobs. The windows were closed and someone hastily had hung blankets from the curtain rods. Two pressure lanterns were burning. One was on the reception desk; the hotel manager carried the other. He was going from window to window for no apparent purpose. Two civilians, RMK people probably, were sitting on the desk. They were wearing trousers only and smoking heavily. Several partially dressed women were clustered in a corner of the lobby.

"A cheerful little group we have," the Frenchman said.

"Where's O'Brien?" the Army sergeant asked. "O'Brien didn't come down with us."

"He beat us down," Davies answered. He put one arm against the wall and rested his head on it.

"Well, where the shit is he? I don't see him around."

"He's outside somewhere," one of the Air America pilots said, the one who wanted to get out of the moneychanging operation. "He fell off the roof in the confusion. He didn't scream or anything, just charged straight off the roof."

"Don't shit me," the sergeant said. "O'Brien's my buddy, he wouldn't come down without me."

"Goddamn it, he fell off the roof."

The Army sergeant sat down on the bottom step of the stairway.

Other people were coming down the stairs, drawn by the light. Knox moved over to the wall by the entrance. All chairs and benches had been stacked against the door. Everyone either stood or squatted dejectedly. Except Davies. He tipped over a stone ash stand filled with sand and sat on it. The manager hurried over, lantern swinging, speaking in excited Vietnamese.

"What does he want," Davies said to the Frenchman.

"He wants you to pay for the mess, what else?"

"Tell him to take a Librium."

"Next he'll be wanting some p for staying here," the taller of the Air America pilots said. He laughed. No one else saw any humor in it so he stopped.

Davies continued to ignore the manager. The manager

finally walked away. The lamp on the reception was beginning to fade. One of the men dressed only in trousers began
pumping up the pressure. They could not hear the pump
strokes because of the muted gunfire which waited in the
distance for them to notice it. They were all sweating. The
lanterns were putting out a lot of heat, but no one minded.

"I've got to get out of here," Knox said.

"Sure you do," Davies said. "We all got to get out of
here."

"You don't see it. I told Rosette I'd be back long before
now. She's probably frightened, really frightened, and wondering where I am."

"Do not worry about this Rosette," the Frenchman said.
"There are at least ten million Viet women you will never
see, much less make love with." He was vastly amused.

"I missed the curfew," the sergeant said.

"I'll write you a letter to Westmoreland."

"People worry about the damndest things," one of the Air
America pilots said. "All I want is getting my young ass out
of here."

"We all want out," Davies said. "Question is, how do we
go about it?"

The big concussions were alternately up very close and
then far away. Maybe even across the river, but there was
the constant stutter of automatic weapons, the whispering
crackle of rockets. A mortar round shook the hotel and
everyone instinctively shielded his head with his hands.
The women were too frightened to scream.

"Just off the end of the porch."

"You think that's just to get the range?"

They sweated for a while. The fighting went on. Planes
flew over and a short time later they heard the flat throaty
boom of heavy bombs.

"Where are they bombing?"

The Frenchman listened intently for a moment. "Cholon."

"Christ, I hope they don't get the moneychangers."

"What kind of planes are those overhead?" the sergeant said.

"Skyraiders," an Air America pilot said. "At least they can operate from Tan son Nhut."

"Well, Tan son Nhut is the safest place around," Davies said.

"We'll go there as soon as it's light."

"What's wrong with right now?"

"And risk running into an ambush? In the daylight we can be identified as Americans."

"The VC can see better, too," the Frenchman said. Nobody had an answer to that.

"I'm not going to Tan son Nhut," Knox said. "I want you to drop me off at my villa."

"Nothing doing. I'm gonna make it from here straight to the base."

"That'll be by Pasteur," the Frenchman said. "That's the best route."

"All right, drop me off someplace along Pasteur. I'll walk the rest of the way."

"Go to your office, or your Embassy."

"I'll go there after I get Rosette."

"She's probably long gone by now."

"I'll do it my way," Knox said. "After all, she hustles the green for us."

"He must have something good going with that cunt."

"There are many good things about Vietnamese women," the Frenchman said. "One is that there are so many of them."

One of the pressure lanterns began to fade and they ceased talking, looking at the waning mist of light and the bare-chested men on the reception trying to pump up the pressure. The light continued to wane, then the mantle spluttered and popped; it failed rapidly then the light was gone except for a brief orange flow from the mantle. Then that too was gone. The man on the reception shook the lantern, then dropped it on the counter top.

They waited and watched the remaining lantern, not looking directly at it because that would hurt their eyes, but to the side, scarcely seeming to breathe when the light flickered once. But it flickered only that one time and they held their collective breaths until they could hold them no longer and let them out in one collective sigh. They watched the slow roll of beaded sweat down the torso of the bare-chested man on the reception and waited for morning inside the shallow cocoon of their own private thoughts and restless fears.

III

The heavy firing receded for a while, then came toward the hotel again. Then the mortars stopped and there was a silence until the machine guns began. "I think we should go out and get O'Brien."

"Go out and get him yourself," Davies said. "I'm not risking my ass for a hunk of dead meat."

"It's not right he should be out there."

No one answered, so they lapsed into silence again, which lasted at least two hours.

Then the Army sergeant started pounding one closed fist into the palm of the other. He did it slowly, and made no sound, but all the same it irritated the rest of them. Though they said nothing. "Damn it, all I can think of is going out and getting O'Brien."

"I'll go with you," the Frenchman said.

"Why?" Davies said.

"So he'll shut up."

"Where you going to put him? You think you can bring a body in here you're crazy."

"We'll put him in one of the rooms upstairs."

"Leave him outside; we'll take him to Tan son Nhut with us."

"How many people do you think you can get in a jeep?"

"Don't count me," the Frenchman said. "I am going to the apartment of a friend on the Rue Catinat."

"That's good thinking," the sergeant said. "If the Cong ever get as far as Tu Do we've lost the war." And then: "I'm gonna go outside for O'Brien. You coming?"

"No. I am going to wait to morning."

"You're backing down. You're going back on your word."

"Not at all."

"You're a rummy Frenchman," said the sergeant.

"You, my friend, are a profiteer."

"Both you pricks hold it down."

"I am sorry I called you a profiteer," said the Frenchman.

"That's okay. I know you didn't mean it.

"I intended to call you a feeder of carrion."

"A buzzard," one of the Air America pilots said. He was plainly delighted. "You meant to call him a buzzard."

"Yes, you are all vultures, you have the word to fit you."

The sergeant got up and went over to the door, where he argued with two houseboys who were sitting on the topmost bench. He shrugged his shoulders and returned. "They won't let me out."

"That's staff-level thinking."

"It's getting light outside."

"The shooting's died down some."

"They're just fighting somewhere else."

"I think I will be well finished with you after today," said the Frenchman.

"You won't go far," Davies said. "There's a lot of money in it."

"Undoubtedly. But I have the satisfaction of calling you vultures."

"Like the man said, you're a rummy goddamn Frenchman."

"Do not start that again. It is almost six o'clock."

"Soon as we can see, we're gonna go."

"What if the jeep's been hit?"

"It won't be."

"But what if it is?"

"It won't be," Davies said fiercely.

"I am glad there is a friend on the Rue Catinat."

"Call me at ConAir when things quiet down."

"Indeed, we shall do business yet."

"If you are still alive," the sergeant said. "And if there is a Rue Catinat still."

"Conspirators are like bitter medicines. They should be taken in small doses, and only when forced."

"Call me when things get back to normal."

"Indeed."

"Let's go."

"You'll drop me off on Pasteur."

Davies did not answer. He checked the main door. The houseboys argued with him, but he brushed them aside and pulled enough furniture out of the way for them to open the door. He peered cautiously out the partially opened door and studied the morning. Then opened it wide enough for one man. "Go out and look for O'Brien."

The sergeant scuttled through the door. Davies flattened himself against the wall. They waited two minutes. Davies pushed the door open further with his foot and started to go out when a mortar exploded close by. He slammed the door and began piling furniture against it. The houseboys helped him. They heard the sergeant run across the porch and bang against the door. Another mortar exploded. Close enough for Knox to fancy he heard the faint cough as the round left its tube.

"For God's sake, let me in."

"We can't, there's too much piled against the door."

"Goddamn you, Davies, let me in, there's no cover out here."

"Find some."

The sergeant cursed.

"You'd better hurry. That porch is exposed," called Davies.

The sergeant cursed, but they heard him turn and run off the porch.

"That was a bastard thing to do," the more sympathetic of the Air America pilots said.

"You want to let him in? Shit, half the North Vietnamese Army could be out there waiting to pour in if we open that door."

They waited until a little past nine o'clock before trying it again. The firing had never really come any closer, and most of the explosions were coming from the direction of Cholon. Davies moved the furniture and opened the door wide, but not so wide he could not close it quickly with his foot. No one volunteered to be first, and he knew enough not to ask anyone. "Don't forget to call me when this is over."

"Indeed," the Frenchman said.

Davies crouched low and crept across the porch. The Air America pilots and Knox followed. They reached the jeep. The sergeant was lying under it. When he slid out his once clean fatigues were spotted with dust rubbed in deeply. Davies unlocked the chain and slid into the seat. The engine was unnaturally loud. Everyone got in. Davies shifted gears and backed out of the parking lot. He let out the clutch with a vengeance and they shot into the street. "I couldn't find O'Brien," the sergeant said.

"I don't think anyone would have moved him."

They drove through the silent and eerily deserted streets. They could hear little above the roar of the engine. Davies did not bother to slow for intersections, but he met no other traffic.

Then they turned off Le Loi past the smoldering wreckage of two American jeeps which had run together. They did not bother to reflect whether it had been an ambush or an accident. Davies drove past the Rex BOQ and the election billboard built over the fishpond. There was a contingent of National Police in front of the Assembly. One of them threw up his carbine and fired one shot at them. Then he dropped the carbine and ran. The others turned to shout something after him. The jeep was on Tu Do now, and they left the Assembly behind. Streaking now past the cathedral and across Thong Nhut.

"There's fighting going on at the Embassy." They all looked, even Davies, but he jerked his eyes back to the street after the briefest of glimpses. Smoke was rising in thin wisps from the compound. Bodies, small as discarded rag dolls, were tumbled here and there in the street. Other dolls were lying down, the better to fire and offer smaller targets. They heard the quick pop-pop of small-arms fire. Knox looked to the left, toward the palace. Two tanks were squatting in front of the gates. One of them had backed into dense coils of concertina wire.

A helicopter buzzed over and tried to land on the roof of the Embassy. The pop-pop of small-arms fire increased; the helicopter slipped to the left, toward the rear of the Embassy. The fire was coming from inside the compound. Knox thought the copter had crashed, but it reappeared

just over the treetops. Then they were across the wide bou-
levard. One more block and then Hong thap Tu. Davies
turned left. "I'll get out here," Knox shouted.

Davies swung over to the curb. "You're a fucking fool."
The jeep was still moving. Knox leaped out and staggered,
falling to one knee before he regained his balance.

IV

Five blocks further on· and only ten minutes before, a fifteen-year-old guerrilla had planted a concussion mine on
Pasteur in hopes of bagging one of the ARVN tanks patrol-
ling around the palace. Two sappers were ready to expose
themselves, then run, in order to draw the tank toward the
mine. But Davies came along first. The mine was made of
explosives taken from an American five-hundred-pound
bomb which had failed to detonate. The fifteen-year-old
guerrilla had painstakingly fashioned it himself, and even
carried it most of the way to Saigon. He was bitterly disappointed that he did not bag a tank. But it was more than
enough to destroy a jeep.

Surprisingly, no one was killed, and they huddled under
the jeep and stayed alive, though the VC took a few desultory shots at them. They were under the jeep for almost
half a day, four people, lying side by side in the heat and
the terror without a word being said between them until a
tank rumbled along late in the afternoon and rescued them.
The VC had moved on by then. Besides, they had used
their one concussion mine. The people under the jeep had
all used the time to think of different stories to tell to explain what had happened.

Duong Tuyen Dau
(The Road to the Front)

THE MAIN HOUSE was still standing. Knox could see the roof and a corner of the house over the wall. A few tiles had been blown loose and the firethorn vine along the corner of the balcony had been ripped away. But that was all. A building across the street was afire and smoke hung thick in the alleyway. The sound of small-arms fire came from the direction of the Embassy, and he heard the high-pitched twitter of a Huey passing overhead. Then its guns stuttered with the arrogant sibilance of ripping cloth.

A ricochet whined somewhere near and Knox instinctively threw up his arm. There was no living person on the street though he could sense people all around. A child was screaming for something, not far away. The sun was only halfway to noon but already he had trouble getting enough oxygen from the hot, stale air. His lungs ached from the effort. There was a sudden cessation of all noise. The baby stopped crying and the firing from the direction of the Embassy died away. Funny, he thought, damned funny. He started to cross the street.

He heard the clack of the helicopter's rotor blades and then saw its shadow playing tag with his own shadow on the bricked street. Little geysers of red dust and singing chips began to fly up from the pavement. My God, they're firing at me, Knox thought, and flung out both arms and waved frantically at the gunship. He missed his footing and fell, twisting his knee badly. His elbow scraped heavily on the bricks and the little geysers flickered steadily where he had just been. Knox gathered his legs and tried to run, but his knee kept folding. His chest labored from the exertion and the fear and the certainty he was going to die. The gunship was turning around and in one hurried glance he could see the vague silhouette of the gunner in the door and the linked belt of the machine gun moving in jerks as the quicksilver bullets reached for him.

"Good God," he said aloud, "good God." Knox wished he could pray. "I never did learn how," he muttered helplessly. Sometimes he remembered all the time he spent not learning how to do things. The shadow of the Huey passed over him and something like a gigantic hand picked him up and slammed him against the brick. His back stung with a hundred individual pinpricks and his mouth was filled with filth from the street. "They're using a grenade launcher, the bastards, can't they see I'm one of them?" Knox said to himself.

Knox started to crawl, but the clatter of rotors was almost directly overhead. He froze into a fetal position. Knees drawn up almost to his chin, one arm sheltering his face. He saw clearly the slow drip of time through the interstices of the clock face on his wrist, each drip falling in his brain like a pebble in a well, concentric spreading rings flowing out until they vanished imperceptibly, and the next one came. The Huey hung momentarily overhead but the geysers of red dust and singing grit did not come. After a moment it lifted away in the direction of the Embassy.

Knox waited. Then raised his head slowly, with infinite cunning. The helicopter was not in sight. A layer of viscous smoke roiled by and he blinked rapidly from the burning, choking tang of it. He rose to a half-crouch and ran for the wall around the courtyard, keeping close to the ground and scuttling like a crab, fantastically alive to the slyness born of desperation and fear. For now he was the whom. Always he had been the who doing the what to the whom. Always the who. And now it was reversed. Something was being done to him and he was desperate.

The courtyard wall funneled him into the alley and suddenly he was between the two big walls and his villa was only a few steps away. The branches and foliage overhead covered him from sight of any prowling helicopter, but he still crouched.

The stippled door of glass sandwiched between the strips of iron was locked. Knox rattled the doorknob and rapped the glass. He remembered the key in his pocket and fumbled for it. In his haste he dropped the brass key and dug frantically in the soil which had spilled from an overturned can of miniature orange bushes until he found it again. He almost dropped it once more, but he got it into the lock somehow and threw the bolt twice.

The ceiling fan in the living room was churning and the curtains were blowing like apparitions. The aquarium was cracked across one end and a thin trickle of water seeped through the rupture. A few bits and pieces of plaster were littered across the floor, and, as he watched, another piece fell into the aquarium. Water sloshed onto the floor and the fish darted in mad confusion about the tank. But the glass held. At least for the time being.

Rosette was lying in bed. The windows were shuttered and the light was dim, but Knox could make out her form under the sheet. She half turned on the bed as if sensing his presence for the first time. She held out her arms and opened them while her back arched and her thighs thrust out toward him. Her eyes were moist in the room's twilight, and he thought she moaned. But he could be sure of nothing.

"What's the matter, Rosette, didn't you hear me banging on the door?"

She did not answer, but thrust her body even further toward him from the rumpled covers. The air conditioner was only faintly audible, and the sheets looked cool. He heard another loud explosion somewhere nearby. Rosette continued to look at him, beseeching him something, he did not know what. Her hips twitched and he slid into bed beside her. Her arms locked around him and fingers dug into the muscles of his shoulders. The pain felt good, refreshing almost after his run across the street.

"One of our own helicopters tried to kill me." He could feel her familiar body through the sheet, and she was moving ever so slightly. The old tingle rippled through his body and he felt himself aroused. He stripped down the sheet and began to kiss her right breast. Rosette inched away from him and he followed. She was moaning again, something low and indistinct which he could not quite hear. One hand sought her leg and he stroked it, knee and thigh.

Knox kissed the smooth, taut skin of her stomach and ran his tongue into her navel. Her entire body convulsed and both hands were now in his hair and along the back of his neck. Her breasts were soiled from the dirt rubbed from his hair. Caressing. He stopped kissing her and exhaled deeply to put his head against her breasts. He moved his body closer to hers and felt her faint heartbeat warm against his ear. Rosette's body jerked. He made soothing noises with his tongue against his teeth the way parents sometimes do to stop a child's crying. He moved his body in rhythm with hers and palpitated her stomach with one hand. He felt himself almost at the point of full arousal and reached across with his other hand to massage her breast and the base of her throat. He heard her teeth chatter together, and her body stiffened, but he was too excited to pay heed. Knox detected a changed pace in her heartbeat and threw off the rest of the sheet to move her leg and kiss the soft inner velvetness of her thighs. The flesh was cool and damp and slightly salty. Her pubic hair tickled his nose.

He continued to arch his body against hers, feeling his manhood rising higher and higher. His breathing was coming in short gasps and he was poised at the peak of excitement. Then he realized her fingers were no longer clutching his hair, and he could no longer feel the beat of her heart in the taut flesh of her stomach. Knox raised his head. Rosette's arms slipped from his shoulders and her eyes were fixed straight ahead at some point behind him. He held an ear against her breast but no answering beat matched the throb in his temple. He called her name, but she did not answer. The sound died into the terrific silence in which he waited.

Rosette's mouth was open slightly and he smelled something faintly sweet, yet bitter, the delicate fragrance of almonds or cloves. Knox took her by both arms and shook her, but her head only lolled awkwardly to one side. His eyes had grown completely accustomed to the dim now, and he saw the subtle fleck of saliva at the corner of her mouth. He leaned forward to brush it away and as he did so he saw the small bluish green jar empty on the bed beneath the edge of pillow.

Dies Irae

AND so he was going back. Sitting in the first-class section of a Pan American jetliner next to a self-made Australian banker from Sidney on his way to Alaska to buy crab meat. Already thirty minutes out of Tan son Nhut. It was pleasant at altitude, the faint whistle of the engines and the reassuring murmur of the stewardess as she moved along the aisle with drinks. The plane was on course for Tokyo. And after that San Francisco.

Already Saigon was two hundred and fifty miles behind him. The land had long since vanished and all that was beneath him was the vast blue reach of some part of the Pacific. The ocean was tranquil; he could see that. On the trip out he had seen whitecaps and the occasional foamed V of a ship's wake. But now everything was somnolent and serene, in fact, lonely. And he looked down with his heart aching when he sat quietly for a moment and chanced to remember how things were, once, and how they might yet have been had not all that happened happened. But his memories were nothing more than recollections of the future.

He thought of B.D. at the airport to see him off, and, curiously, he was sympathetic for B.D.'s obese figure, made ludicrous by the large, muddy, once white cast on one leg. There had been no difficulty in breaking his contract. No

talk of cowardice or even his reasons. No attempt to dis-
suade him. Everything done automatically. As if it were an
everyday occurrence, even to the handshake from Mister
Balfour, who came over from the damaged Embassy Annex
to say good-bye. Other than that his departure had been little noticed.

Knox left with his parents' telegraphed money order for
first-class passage and B.D.'s sympathy for him as much as
his for B.D. Carrying the fatalistic knowledge like a talis-
man, that he had failed even at failing; hated himself twice,
once for the attempt, and again for failing. Because no one
really cared, not really. Then again, he did not even care if
he failed. And thus he had failed again. Not achieving recognition as a failure was the ultimate, absolute failure.
Even B.D., just back from Manila, standing with the aid of
a cane, his hand half-lifted as if to bid farewell, then thinking better of it, turning to melt easily into the restive, en-
vious crowd, even he had not admitted recognizing Knox's
failure. Though Knox knew B.D. had seen it.

God knows, it had been difficult enough getting a seat on
one of the first civilian flights out of Tan son Nhut, but the
Mission had stepped in and taken care of that. Smoothly.
Nothing required on his part. Just their request and that
was that. He could not have made the arrangements himself. He remembered someone once, a long time ago it
seemed, who was packing a suitcase and crying as she
packed. When he had finally asked her how she could do
this to him she had told him that a great many things had
happened to her during the year she was married to him,
and nothing much could touch her anymore. He remembered saying that he never wanted to get that way, and she
looked at him and said, "Nobody wants to, but you will."
The circle was vicious, but it was only another name for a
descending spiral.

The stealthy knowledge carried to the heart that he had succeeded only in trading one scar for another. Leaving. Yearning for no place in particular, a remembrance of events that never quite happened, of lives not really touched. A surrealistic finality that the only war he had fought was the war with himself, and he had never been in any danger of winning that. Even though war was the most democratic experience known to mankind because it equalized both oppressor and victim.

Something had been produced, but plainly not fun, nor excitement, nor fulfillment. Wondering why fun was always elsewhere, never where he was. But the fun quest was an ordeal, and he felt jaded. Spent. The package was empty, even though what had once been unprofitable was now profitable. At any price those who had too clear a conscience had to be kept from living and dying in peace. Or even the pleasures (or the right) of sleeping soundly of a night. Even those in higher places, who long ago had learned how not to realize that they did not mind sleeping at night. Knox had forgotten long ago what it was to even miss sleep or a step.

The stewardess was at his side, offering him a choice of drinks from an assortment on the cart she was pushing.

"No, thank you," he said sharply.

"Is there anything wrong? Do you feel ill? Perhaps you would like an aspirin." The stewardess spoke in the carefully cultivated tones of her stewardess school, and with the smug knowledge that by merely flying into Saigon once a month she could take a bigger income tax deduction.

"No, I'm all right." He tried to smile but his lips were tight. "I've just had a rough time in 'Nam."

"Oh?" Her voice was all concern. "Were you in the Tet fighting?"

"Nguyen dan Tet?" He used the full name, but unknowingly reversed it, hoping it would impress her. Suddenly, obscurely, he hoped it would. There were no military or government people in the first-class section, at least as far as he could tell. Everyone looked like tourists or businessmen. "Yes, I was right in the thick of it. I wasn't three blocks from the Embassy when everything broke loose."

"Were you in Vietnam very long?" She had forgotten about the drinks and another passenger further forward in the cabin swiveled to glare back in irritation.

"Too long," Knox said.

"Stewardess, if he doesn't want a drink what about pushing that damn cart up this way? Some of the rest of us might be thirsty." The passenger turned back to his seat angrily.

The stewardess smiled tentatively as if to excuse herself and began to move away. "Miss?" She stopped. "Perhaps when you have time you would bring me that aspirin. And I will take a gin and tonic. The doctors say it's good for my malaria." She mixed his drink hurriedly and inexpertly, using far too much gin and glancing at the passenger further up the aisle from the corner of her eye.

She handed him the gin and tonic. "I'll be by later with the aspirin," she said, and moved away with the cart. Knox hoped she would return and talk to him. The Australian waited until she was out of earshot, then folded his paper. He had been reading an Australian newspaper which had a large picture of General Loan of the National Police with a small pistol in his hand, taken just at the moment that a Viet Cong street terrorist was eternally being shot. Knox looked at the photograph for a long moment, but did not feel anything.

"Pardon my asking," the Australian banker said in his

clipped accent. "But what's it really like in Veet Nam? According to the papers that Tet thing was a bit of a bloody blue."

"Like nothing you ever dreamed of. It's the only place in the world where you can have diarrhea and a dusty asshole at the same time."

"That's a corkin' beaut." The Australian looked startled for a moment, but then he laughed. He dug Knox in the ribs with his elbow. "You keep that shelia entertained with a few ditties like that and she'll go whacko."

Knox leaned back in his seat and took a sip of his drink. It really had far too much gin in it. No matter.

"When she comes back I'll hit the kick for you." The Australian lapsed back into his newspaper. He read for a few minutes and slowly shook his head. "This thing really has you blokes up a gum tree."

Knox did not reply. He was trying to appear laconic, but he stirred irritably in his seat and took only token sips of his gin and tonic. The big plane slipped effortlessly through the high clear sky, gracefully and silently picking up the frozen invisible miles from somewhere in front of the plane and just as effortlessly replacing them after it had passed as if nothing had happened. But of course something had. A gigantic assemblage of complex plates of aluminum, chromium, hundreds of miles of wires and cables, intricate devices to propel it in one direction and other devices to tell it where it was in reference to space and time and position, hot turbine blades spewing the fumes of burned kerosene into the compliant sky, and over one hundred people entombed within the shiny aluminum walls, hung suspended by the most gossamer of threads above an abyss which no one could see, or having seen it could recognize for what it was.

Of a certainty something had happened. They had been there and passed, even if they could not tell it. The air which moved aside for their passage could tell it. The skein of exhausted kerosene would hold the story of their passage for any who could read it. And the passengers would record within themselves the subtle changes of having been there, even if they had not known where they were or what they were doing, or much less cared. It was all there, rolling and unrolling in the thin cold air of twenty-seven thousand feet. Though they would never realize it. It would know them. They were always in the same familiar places they could never locate.

Already an hour gone out of Saigon. The Indochinese coast far away in time and infinity. Almost as if it had never happened. The Gypsy Bar. The house on Tran cao Van not far from the zoo, or the Embassy. The ineptitudes of his fellow agents. All of it. Even the easy way CAS had let him go. Perhaps they really did know more than he credited them with knowing. But he doubted that. He did not know where he was going. But that did not matter. He did not know where he had been. And having been there he had not recognized it because he had been expecting something else. Just what, he had no conception, and therefore would not have recognized it anyway. But he had been. That was the main thing. For after all, a man was the sum of his passions. Though the height of a man's wisdom is that he knows when he does not know. Knox never knew when he did not know.

He had capital for a lot of conversation now. Yes, posturing as well. Closely attuned to the old Chinese saying that he who loses is a brigand, while he who pulls it off is a prince. Even though he had not lost he had not pulled it off, either. But he could talk it out. He always had. It did not matter who won or lost, or even how the game was played, only who kept score. Perhaps he could start with the stewardess.

A little more than an hour out of Saigon and already it was another world. Another time. Ahead was Tokyo. And after that San Francisco. And after that . . .

FINI